Praise for Ally

5 Coffee Cups! "...This is the most beautiful and soul touching story I have read in a long time. Ms. Blue created these two exceptional characters with tragic histories and brought them together. Extremely well written, this story will touch anyone who have been in similar circumstances. Although tearful at times, this tale has spicy hot sex scenes and extraordinary instances when you are cheering these two men on. This is a must read, but have tissues handy." ~ *Wateena, Coffee Time Romance*

5 Blue Ribbons! "WILLOW BEND is a poignantly sweet tale of love and loss. I have to say that it's too bad there aren't more towns like the one depicted in this book, where not only is the gay lifestyle accepted within the community, but people genuinely care for each other. ...Ally Blue does an amazing job taking us through the emotional roller coaster that goes along with the loss of a loved one. You'll experience each of the emotions as well as share in the triumphs and disappointments. I'd suggest having a box of tissues nearby. There's nothing quite like being able to smile through your tears." ~ *Chrissy Dionne, Romance Junkies Reviewer*

"...amazing book by Ally Blue. The characters seemed to reach right out and pull you into their lives. Paul is a man who desperately wants to hold onto a lost love, until a new love opens his eyes. Cory is a man dedicated and loving in every possible way. A very well written story that will capture your heart and win you over right away. A big two thumbs up to Ally Blue. I highly recommend this book." ~ *Shay, Sensual Reads and Reviews*

4 Stars! If you like M/M sex then this one is for you. If you are looking for a story with some beautiful relationships enhanced by sex, Willow Bend is for you. Paul and Cory had some pretty steamy scenes together. Their love for each other unfolds gradually and is revealed in many different ways. Loss of a loved one is handled realistically and sensitively. I loved the way Ms. Blue accurately portrayed how people feel with a loss. The town of Willow Bend with a few exceptions was quite accepting of their love...Willow Bend is a wonderful story. I will be looking forward to reading more by Ally Blue. Great job!! ~ *Elise, eCataromance Reviews*

4 Stars! HOT "Willow Bend is definitely a tearjerker. It is sentimental and heart-wrenching...The good writing, wonderful characters and emotionally charged drama helped me to enjoy Willow Bend immensely. I would gladly read more of Ally Blue's work, if for no other reason than to experience a good cry." ~ *Suni Farrar, Just Erotic Romance Reviews*

WILLOW BEND

Ally Blue

A Samhain Publishing, Ltd. publication.

Samhain Publishing, Ltd.
2932 Ross Clark Circle, #384
Dothan, AL 36301

Willow Bend
Copyright © 2006 by Ally Blue
Cover by Scott Carpenter
Print ISBN: 1-59998-215-3
Digital ISBN: 1-59998-062-2
www.samhainpublishing.com

First Samhain Publishing, Ltd. electronic publication: May 2006
First Samhain Publishing, Ltd. print publication: August 2006

ABOUT ALLY BLUE

To learn more about Ally Blue, please visit http://www.allyblue.com/ Send an email to Ally Blue at ally@allyblue.com or join her Yahoo! group to join in the fun with other readers as well as Ally! http://groups.yahoo.com/group/loveisblue

DEDICATION

For my husband, who is always proud of me and has supported me all along.

CHAPTER ONE

"Sir? We're here."

Paul Gordon opened his eyes, pushed his shaggy dark hair out of his face, and blinked up at the smiling young woman hovering over him. For a second he couldn't remember where he was. Then it all came back. He was on an airplane, which had just landed in Savannah, Georgia, clear across the country from the only home he'd ever known. His stomach knotted.

"Thanks." He gave the flight attendant a tight smile. She nodded briskly and moved off again.

Paul yawned and stretched, trying to ease his cramped muscles. Airline seats just weren't made for people over six feet tall. He stood, tugged his single bag out of the overhead bin, and edged his way down the aisle.

Thirty minutes later, Paul sat slouched in the back of a cab, heading down a narrow ribbon of road that stretched straight and level as far as the eye could see. He gazed out the window at the flat expanse of pines and grassy marshes. The ninety-eight degree heat rose in shimmering waves from the winding waterways on either side of the road. All his life he'd been surrounded by the city, with the craggy peaks of the Northern Rockies flung against the sky in the background. This horizon, which stretched into infinity, made him feel off balance.

The trip to the little town of Willow Bend, South Carolina passed in silence, broken only by the cheery pop blaring from the radio. Paul didn't mind. He'd never been crazy about making small talk with strangers in the first place. Right then, he thought he'd rather be drawn and quartered than have a conversation with anyone.

The driver turned off the main road just short of the town center, took a couple more turns and pulled into a long gravel drive, the last one on the dead-end road. Paul sat up and peered curiously at the little cottage half-hidden by oak trees and oleander. A red metal roof and wide, shady porch peeked out from between the leaves. He'd bought it without even seeing a picture, and this first sight of his new home stirred an unfamiliar excitement in him.

The driver put the car in park and slung a thick, deeply tanned arm over the back of the seat. "That'll be seventy-five, hon."

Paul dug a hundred dollar bill out of his wallet and laid it in the woman's outstretched hand. "Keep the change."

Her lined face broke into a grin. "Thank you very much. You have a good stay. And you just call and ask for Edna when you get ready to head back, hear?"

He slid out of the car, hefting his bag onto his shoulder. "I don't plan on going back. Thanks anyway."

He shut the door and turned away before she could say anything else. A moment later he heard the crunch of wheels on gravel as the taxi rolled back down the drive. Then he was alone, for the first time in what felt like forever. He dropped his bag on the porch, sat on the big wooden rocker and just soaked up the silence. The only sounds were the drone of insects and the occasional trill of a bird. He made up his mind to explore the tree-shaded grounds the next morning.

Not that it was going to take him long to unpack and get settled. He'd only brought what he considered the bare necessities—a few changes of clothes, a toothbrush, soap, and his painting supplies. Most of what he owned he'd given away, preferring to start his new life completely fresh. A new place, new people, new things. Nothing to bring back painful memories.

Of course, the second he thought that, the memories came, overwhelming him with a sadness that had become all too familiar. The sudden buzz of his cell phone was an unexpected but welcome distraction. He flipped it open.

"Hi, Mom," he said, smiling.

Cheryl Gordon's musical laugh sounded over the phone. "How'd you know it was me?"

"Nobody else has this number. What's up?"

"Nothing, I just wanted to make sure you got there okay."

"The flight was fine. I'm at the house right now."

"Oh, good. Is it nice?"

"Don't know. Haven't been inside yet." He looked around at the cheerful yellow exterior walls and neatly trimmed lawn. "The outside's cute, though. Nice, big covered porch. Lots of trees. I'm gonna go have a look around in the morning."

"Good, I'm glad it's a nice place." He heard the relief in his mother's voice. "Honey, are you sure about this?"

"Mom, if I wasn't sure, I wouldn't have bought the place."

"I know. But it hasn't been all that long, really, maybe you should come back and let me—"

"No," Paul interrupted. "Look, Mom, I know you want to help. But I'm fine now. Honest. You don't need to take care of me anymore."

"But, Paul—"

"Mom, it's been more than a year. I'm tired of everybody coddling me. I can look after myself. And I...I really just need to be alone."

"Sweetheart, I don't mean to be a pest. I'm sure you'll be just fine. But you're my baby and I worry."

Paul laughed. "Mom, I'm thirty-two. When am I going to stop being your baby?"

"Never." Cheryl sighed. "Well, I suppose you want to go now and get acquainted with your new place."

"Kind of, yeah. But I'm glad you called. Love you, Mom. Say hi to Dad for me."

"I will. Love you too, sweetheart. Call me, okay?"

"Sure thing. Bye."

"Bye."

Paul snapped his cell phone closed then sat lost in thought for several minutes. Finally he levered himself to his feet, picked up his bag, fished out the key the realtor had mailed him and let himself into his new home.

The inside turned out to be as neat and pretty as the outside. He'd paid a great deal extra to buy the furniture and appliances as well, and the place didn't disappoint. The furniture was plain but comfortable, and the wood floor looked freshly waxed. Simple, pale blue curtains covered the many windows. A short hallway led to a large, bright kitchen, complete with deep cabinets, an old but sturdy white refrigerator and a little wooden table with two chairs. Through a doorway beside the refrigerator lay a small screened-in back porch.

A door on the left side of the hallway opened into a surprisingly large bedroom. The walls were painted a soft, peaceful blue. The old-fashioned iron frame of the queen-sized bed was painted white. A large wooden dresser sat against the wall opposite the bed. In the corner, between the two big windows, a full-length swivel mirror in an oak stand reflected the early evening light.

Paul found the tiny bathroom, with its pedestal sink and claw-foot tub, tucked into a narrow space between the bedroom and living room. One door opened into the hallway, the other into the bedroom. Sunshine filtered in through a small, frosted window set high in the wall opposite the hall door. Paul grinned at the bright room.

Within ten minutes, he'd unpacked his few belongings, leaving the painting supplies in the duffle bag until he could find the best place for them. He breathed a silent thank you to the former owners when he realized that the elderly couple had left him not only a coffee maker, but a bag of ground coffee and a small wicker basket full of apples. A note on the kitchen table told him they'd left the pickup truck—which he'd also bought—in the barn. The keys to the truck sat on top of the note.

He ate one of the apples and a bag of pretzels he'd saved from the plane, then filled the antique tub and soaked until the water went cold. The cross-country flight and long taxi ride had left him aching all over. Fourteen months and change after the car crash that had almost killed him, he could still feel all the places where his bones had been broken.

Eventually he climbed out of the tub, pulled on a pair of ragged shorts and wandered out to the front porch. He sat rocking as dusk deepened into night, breathing in clean, humid air tinged with a hint of the nearby ocean. Crickets and bullfrogs filled the night with a lilting music. Watching the fireflies winking in the trees, Paul felt a peace like he hadn't known since the night of the accident. The night his whole life had fallen apart.

He sighed and rubbed his eyes. *Maybe one day I'll be able to get through twenty-four hours without thinking of it.*

"Not fucking likely," he muttered to the shadowed yard.

Suddenly the dark seemed oppressive. He headed back inside, shutting the door on the night. Almost two hours later, he finally dozed off, curled up in the middle of the bare mattress. The lamp beside the bed burned all night.

CHAPTER TWO

The next morning dawned bright and hot. Paul stood barefoot on the thin grass of the backyard, sipping coffee while he watched the sun rise over the trees in the distance. Only a few feet past the back porch, the oaks gave way to a field of yellow-green grass that rippled in the hot breeze. A thin strip of pines stood on the other side of the wide meadow. He could smell the faint salt tang of the nearby ocean.

Paul squinted in the harsh early morning light. He felt tired and wrung out from the long trip the day before and from another restless night. His left hip throbbed where the speeding sports car had smashed the driver's side door into his body, splitting the upper part of his femur nearly in half. He rubbed absently at it for a moment, then turned and limped back into the house.

Half an hour later, he locked the house and headed out to the barn. It lay not far from the house, in a wide clearing down a narrow path between the oleanders. At first glance, it looked a little forbidding— a silent hulk of a building, red paint graying in the merciless sun. But closer inspection showed the place to be perfectly sound.

He wandered inside, gazing curiously around him. The cool dimness of the interior felt soothing, relaxing. Peaceful. Ignoring the old green pickup truck for a moment, he made his way up the ladder at the back of the barn. What he saw at the top brought a big grin to his face.

"Oh, fuck me," Paul whispered. "This is it. It's perfect."

The empty loft was huge, the ceiling high enough to offer a sense of space but not so high that it would be difficult to heat in the winter. Old-fashioned double doors stood closed on the far end. Motes of dust floated lazily in the rays of sunlight that shone through the cracks in the wood. Even in the half-light, he could see the possibilities.

He paced the length and breadth of the sturdy wooden floor, already planning in his mind. *This could work. Put a big window where those doors are. Maybe a skylight overhead. It's a perfect place for my new art studio.* He did his best to ignore the sharp pang that stabbed him at the thought. The past was gone. He had to concentrate on the future now.

He pushed the looming memories firmly to the back of his mind, then climbed back down the ladder and headed for the house. A quick search of his bag turned up the pen and small spiral notebook that he carried with him everywhere. He hurried back to the barn loft, where he spent nearly an hour building his studio in his mind and jotting down a list of things he would need.

He couldn't help smiling as he tucked the list into his pocket and climbed back down the ladder. He hadn't felt this excited about anything in a long time. Despite his assurances to his mother the night before, he'd been terrified of moving. He'd done it because he simply couldn't stay in Spokane any longer, but he'd never been sure that moving would actually help. Now, it seemed as though the inner voice urging him to leave had been right. This place could be really good for him. Give him the chance he needed to start over.

The old truck's engine roared to life as soon as he turned the key. He backed carefully out of the barn and rolled down the driveway. His stomach turned over at the thought of having to face the inevitable curiosity of the townspeople, but he had to do it at some point. Might as well get it over with.

After a couple of wrong turns, he found his way back to the main road into Willow Bend. The little town was unexpectedly charming, its streets shaded by the gnarled, ancient willows that gave it its name. Brick planters full of colorful flowers decorated each corner, and the sidewalks teemed with a surprising variety of people.

Paul wasn't sure what he'd expected. Weathered old men playing chess on the general store porch, probably. Those old men were there, along with their wives gossiping on the wooden benches. But there were children too, laughing as they ran down the sidewalks. Young couples strolled hand in hand, gazing in shop windows. Paul did a double take when he saw two middle-aged women holding hands at an outdoor table in front of a French-style cafe. As he watched, one leaned over and kissed the other lightly on the lips. Nobody seemed to take any notice, as if it were an everyday thing.

Maybe it is. He smiled as he pulled the truck into an empty parking space. Maybe he wouldn't have to be as careful as he'd been afraid he might. He squelched that line of thought immediately. A gay-friendly community would be great, yes. But it didn't matter, because he wasn't going to be dating.

Never? the nagging voice in the back of his head prodded. *What, you planning to spend the rest of your life alone? He wouldn't have wanted that and you know it.*

"Shut up," Paul hissed. He closed his eyes, leaned his head against the back of the seat, and just breathed for a minute. When the knot in his guts loosened a little, he climbed out of the truck and set out to look for the things he would need to convert an old barn loft into an art studio.

🄰   🄰   🄰

By noon, he had the bed of the truck loaded up with everything from an easel to an air conditioner. The rumble in his stomach reminded him that he hadn't eaten anything since the evening before. After a moment's thought, he decided to go get some lunch before heading to the grocery store. He locked the camper top that covered the back of the pickup and set off down the street again.

A tip from the sweet-faced elderly woman at the hardware store counter led him to a restaurant on the edge of town. The sign out front read Uncle Charlie's Porch. A wide, covered porch ran all the way around the large, rambling log building. The parking lot was packed, but the place was so big that Paul only had to wait a couple of minutes for a table. He lowered himself into the sturdy wooden chair with a sigh and gazed out the window at the creek winding its way through the marsh grass.

"Hi," said a voice at his side. "I'm Cory, I'll be your server today."

Paul turned and looked up into the biggest, greenest eyes he'd ever seen. The eyes twinkled above a snub nose dusted with freckles and a wide, sensual mouth. Chestnut curls streaked with sun-bleached copper brushed the curve of the boy's shoulder. Paul stared.

The young man smiled, showing deep dimples. "Can I get you a drink?"

"Uh." Paul gazed up at the green eyes, feeling a little flustered. "Um, tea, please."

"Hot or iced?"

Paul blinked. "What?"

Cory's smile widened. Paul shocked himself by wondering if the boy's slender body had the same golden tan as his face. "You can get tea either hot or on ice here. Sorry, I figured you're from up north someplace. Some people from up north have never heard of iced tea. Sort of depends on where they're from, I guess."

"You're partly right." Paul grinned, relieved at having found his voice at last. "I'm from Washington, but I know all about iced tea."

"Washington State, you mean?"

"Yeah. Spokane."

"Wow. Long way to come for a vacation."

Paul took a deep breath. "I'm not on vacation. I just moved here."

Cory's eyes locked with Paul's, and Paul felt a thrill go through him. Something in that sharp gaze said that maybe, just maybe...

Paul shook himself. Even if Cory was interested, he wasn't. Couldn't be.

"Well, I sure hope you like it here," Cory said. "So, what about that tea, huh?"

"Let me have the iced tea. Unsweetened."

"Got it." Cory gave Paul a look he couldn't quite figure out. "Be right back."

Cory turned and strolled off. Paul couldn't help watching the graceful way his body moved, the muscles of his thighs and ass bunching in the tight black pants. Feelings he'd thought long dead stirred at the sight. It had been so long since he'd touched a man. So long since he'd been touched, or kissed. So long since the last time he and Jay had made love, the afternoon before that fateful night. Before that drunk driver had taken Jay's life, and left Paul's shattered.

"Here you go."

Paul started at the sound of Cory's voice. Cory grinned as he set down a tall glass full of iced tea. "Oh. Thanks," Paul said. He gave Cory a shaky smile.

"Sure thing." Cory pulled a pad out of his pocket. "You ready to order, or you need a minute?"

Paul glanced down at the menu he hadn't even opened yet. "What would you recommend?"

Cory's eyes narrowed in thought, plump lips pursing. Paul swallowed.

"The crab salad sandwich," Cory said. "It's the best you'll find anyplace."

Paul smiled. "Sounds great."

"Yeah." Cory held Paul's gaze for an endless second, then turned and walked off.

🔲 🔲 🔲

"Crab salad sandwich." Cory tore the top sheet off his order pad and slapped it onto the counter. The chef waved at him without turning her attention from the sauce she was stirring.

Cory poured himself a glass of ice water and drank the whole thing in one breath. He felt a little off-kilter. Uncle Charlie's Porch was the most popular restaurant for miles around. Everybody ate there, and he'd waited on some pretty hot guys before without getting all worked up about it. But this one... Damn. This one was something else. Tall and slim. Smooth, olive-toned skin. Jet black hair falling carelessly around a thin, serious face softened by thoroughly kissable lips. Eyes so pale blue they were almost white, fringed with lashes like black lace. Something in those eyes tugged at Cory's heart and captured his mind like nothing else had in a long time.

"Hey, Cory!" Alicia Trask bounced up, giving him a big grin as she set her order on the counter. "What's up?"

"Nothing. Just taking a little breather." He grinned back at her.

She widened her clear brown eyes at him. "Oh, please. Who is he?"

"Who's who?"

"Whoever's got you all hot and bothered." Alicia nodded toward Cory's section, brown pigtails bobbing. "That him, the one with the black hair?"

Cory started to deny it, then decided, what the hell. Alicia would figure it out anyhow. "Yeah, that's him."

"Pretty."

"Tell me about it." Cory stared at the man's profile, admiring his sculpted, almost classical beauty. "Think he'd go out with me?"

Alicia chuckled as she filled glasses and set them on a large round tray. "You know anybody who wouldn't?"

"C'mon, I'm serious. You think he would?"

"I'm serious too, stupid. Every straight girl and gay guy in town wants to get with you. Hell, I'd go out with you if you didn't have that thing between your legs."

Cory laughed. "Dyke."

"Better believe it, boy. Give me the fairer sex any day."

Cory stared thoughtfully at the side of the man's face. "Doesn't matter anyhow. He's probably straight."

"Why don't you find out?" Alicia raised her eyebrows at him as she headed out to serve drinks.

"Maybe I will," Cory called after her. He filled a plastic pitcher with water, and another with iced tea, to make the rounds of his tables and refill the glasses. "Yeah. Maybe I will."

A group of twelve tourists came in not ten minutes later, and since Cory was the only one with two tables free to put together, he got them. After that, he had his hands full keeping the iced tea and root beer flowing while keeping up with all his other tables as well. Not that he minded so much. He liked waiting on the kids in particular. They were excited to be eating out and easy to please.

At one point, while helping a little boy in a Batman T-shirt decide what he wanted for dessert, Cory looked up and saw the black-haired stranger watching him. The man's eyes burned with a tangible longing. Those pale eyes quickly shifted back to the half-eaten sandwich in front of him, but not fast enough to hide his obvious attraction. Cory's pulse sped up.

Cory kept one eye on the black-haired man while he worked. Finally, the man popped the last bite of crab salad into his mouth and sat back with a sigh. Cory ran a hand through his unruly curls and approached the table with his most dazzling smile in place.

"How was everything?" he asked, topping off the man's glass.

"Wonderful." The blue eyes beamed up at him. "You were right, that crab salad is the best I've ever tasted. Thank you."

"My pleasure. You want some dessert? Our key lime pie is out of this world."

"Sounds great, but I'm stuffed. Maybe another time."

"I hope so." Cory set the bill face down on the table. "I'll take that whenever you're ready."

21

"I'm ready now." He reached into the back pocket of his shorts, pulled out his wallet, and handed Cory a twenty. "Keep the change."

Cory stared. That came out to about a forty percent tip. "Wow. Thanks."

"Sure." The man stood, grimacing a little and favoring his left hip. "Pleasure meeting you, Cory."

"Yeah, you too." Cory watched as the man started to move away. He felt like he was missing something. Suddenly it struck him, and he hurried to catch up. "Hey, wait."

The stranger stopped and gave him a curious look. "Yes?"

Cory looked at the floor, shy suddenly. "Um. It's just, I don't know your name."

"Paul. I'm Paul Gordon."

Cory glanced back up and was mildly surprised to see Paul smiling at him. "Cory Saunders. Pleased to meet you, Paul." He stuck out his hand and they shook.

"Same here," Paul answered.

Cory grinned. "Maybe I'll see you around sometime?"

Paul pinned Cory with a look that made him feel hot all over. "I hope so."

Then he was gone, striding out the door with a hint of a limp. Cory stared after him for a while before shaking himself out of his lust-induced stupor to check on his remaining customers.

The rest of the afternoon and evening flew by in a constant rush of hungry patrons. Cory didn't mind. More customers meant more tips, and he needed the money. Plus it kept his mind off Paul. He had a feeling that not thinking about Paul was going to be difficult.

After the restaurant closed for the night, Cory said goodbye to Alicia as she headed for her car, and bent to unlock the chain on his bicycle. His mother's battered old Buick had given out on him more than five months before and he hadn't had the money to fix it. Luckily the little house where he and his mother lived was only five miles from Uncle Charlie's Porch. It wasn't a bad ride, unless it rained. He dreaded winter, when the rain would be just as frequent, but cold.

A clear late June evening, though, was a wonderful time to pedal a bike along the flat, shady roads. At nine-thirty dark was just beginning to fall, and the fierce heat had dissipated enough that the air felt wonderfully cool against his face. He let his mind drift as he pedaled, too tired to focus on any one thing, not even the memory of Paul's smile. Wednesday was his double-shift day, working breakfast through dinner without a break, and he was exhausted.

LaNelle Harrison's car still sat in the rutted dirt driveway when Cory got home. He breathed a sigh of relief. Sometimes she had to go before he got home, leaving his mother alone. Nothing had ever happened, but it made him nervous anyway.

"Hi, Mrs. Harrison." Cory pulled the screen door shut behind him and hurried through the tiny kitchen into the living room. "How's Mama?"

"Pretty good." The slender black woman pushed herself up from the sagging couch and switched the TV off. "I did her tube feeding 'bout an hour ago, so she's pretty much set for the night. She gets her seizure medicine at midnight, and the steroid at four."

"Okay, thanks."

The woman patted the neat gray bun at the nape of her neck. "Cory, honey, you know I don't like to push you, but..."

"Yeah, I know." Cory hadn't paid Mrs. Harrison for the last two weeks. Getting the refrigerator repaired when it had broken down had used up every bit of money he'd had. He dug a wad of bills out of his pocket and handed it to her. "That's sixty bucks. I'll pay you the rest Friday, soon as I get my check."

Her dark eyes fixed him with a sharp look. "Baby, this is everything you made today, ain't it?"

"No," he lied. She raised a skeptical eyebrow, and he forced a grin. "Really good tips today." At least that part was true.

She pursed her lips, clearly not believing him. But she put the money in her purse anyway. That suited Cory fine. She needed the money too, her only other income being from her social security, which wasn't much.

He and the retired RN had a good arrangement. She took care of his mother while he worked, and he paid her what he could, helping out in other ways to make up the difference. He'd built a new wheelchair ramp for her paraplegic husband all by himself, something he took great pride in.

"All right," Mrs. Harrison said. "I got to head home. My James'll be looking for me. What time you need me tomorrow?"

"Not 'til noon. I gotta fix a couple things around here, so Kevin's taking the morning group out tomorrow. I'm taking the one o'clock group, then I've got dinner shift at Charlie's." His spirits rose at the thought of his part-time job leading sea kayak tours to nearby Otter Island. He loved being out on the water, even herding tourists around.

Mrs. Harrison shook her head. "You work too much, honey. Gonna wear yourself down."

"I don't mind." He plopped down on a cracked plastic chair and stretched, popping joints.

"You're a good boy, Cory. Taking care of your mama and all."

He gave her a tired smile. "Couldn't do it without you, Mrs. Harrison."

She smiled back at him. "Well, you get a good night's rest, you hear? Tomorrow I'll bring you some of the green beans and fig preserves I put up."

"Sounds great, thanks." Cory waved as Mrs. Harrison slung her purse over her shoulder and made her way down the steps from the kitchen door, carefully avoiding the broken top step.

She'd left him a big bowl of her homemade vegetable soup, plus some cucumbers and tomatoes from her garden. He laughed quietly. She knew he got a discount at the restaurant, but she never failed to leave him some of whatever she'd brought for her own dinner. He stuck an experimental finger in the soup. Still warm. He grabbed a spoon from the dish drain and headed down the short hallway to the bedroom.

Lorraine Saunders lay on her back with the big foam wedge under her upper body to keep her tube feeding from coming back up. Her short brown hair was neatly combed, and she had on a fresh nightgown. Mrs. Harrison must've bathed her. Cory would've done it if he needed to, but he was glad he didn't have to. It wasn't a difficult job, his mother being a tiny, delicate woman even before the brain tumor that had left her comatose. But it broke his heart every time, seeing the wasting of her once strong muscles, the bed sores that popped up all the time in spite of his best efforts to prevent them.

"Hi, Mama." He planted a kiss on her forehead, sat on the chair he kept beside her bed, and started wolfing down soup. "I met someone today. Real nice guy. And man, was he gorgeous. Think I might ask him out."

She didn't so much as twitch an eyelash. He hadn't expected her to. It had been more than a month since the last time she'd spoken to him, or opened her eyes. But he couldn't help hoping.

He finished his soup in silence, staring out the window into the darkness and thinking of all the work waiting for him in the morning. The air conditioner in Mama's room needed fixing. Because of work, he hadn't had a chance since it broke down two days before, so that came first. Then there was the broken step outside the kitchen door. And that leak under the bathroom sink that kept coming back no matter how many times he thought he'd fixed it. And just to top it off, the leak in his front bicycle tire was getting worse. He'd patched it so many times he'd lost count. He'd need a new tube pretty soon.

Cory sighed, hauled himself out of the chair, and shuffled back into the kitchen to wash the bowl and spoon. Sometimes it bothered him, how the work never seemed to end. How his life had become a treadmill of working, looking after Mama and trying to keep the old house from falling apart around their ears. He was twenty-four years old; he should be in college, or starting an exciting career or at least partying on the weekends. Not working two jobs just to keep the lights on, keep himself fed and pay someone to take care of Mama. Sometimes he wished...

"Stop that, Cory," he ordered himself. "You don't wish that. You know you don't."

And he didn't, not really.

Except sometimes, he did.

CHAPTER THREE

Paul had been in his new home almost a week before he remembered he needed to buy clothes.

He'd been working like a demon for days, getting the art studio in shape, and nothing else had managed to hold his attention for long. The Monday after his arrival in Willow Bend, the old barn loft had begun to look like a real studio, and Paul had run out of clothes that weren't covered in dirt and paint. He stood naked in front of the washing machine on the back porch and silently cursed himself for not buying laundry detergent.

He frowned at the black clouds gathering outside. The prospect of driving into town in the downpour obviously coming didn't appeal to him. But he had nothing to wear that wasn't filthy, and nothing to wash the dirty clothes with, so it looked like a trip to town was unavoidable.

"Shit." Paul sighed, turned around and trudged back into his bedroom. He pulled on the clothes he'd just spent all morning working in and went to find the truck keys.

🔲 🔲 🔲

By mid-afternoon he had five bags full of jeans, shorts, and shirts, a couple pairs of sneakers, some sandals, and a box of laundry detergent. His hip ached in that peculiar way that only came from shopping. Days on end of hard labor in his emerging studio hardly bothered him at all, but three hours of shopping made him hurt worse than he had in a while. He grimaced as he slung the bags into the space behind the driver's seat and then climbed behind the wheel.

He glanced at his watch. Almost four o'clock. His stomach grumbled, reminding him he'd forgotten to eat that day. Again. The thought of food made him remember Uncle Charlie's Porch. Which, of course, made him think of Cory.

Again.

Coming home from the restaurant last week, he hadn't been able to think of anything else. Those big green eyes, that wide smile. The sexy way the boy moved. And Cory was clearly interested. The way the young man looked at him made him burn.

He'd drifted on fantasies of what it would feel like to kiss Cory, to caress that golden skin. Until he'd gotten home, and gone into his bedroom. And seen Jay's picture.

Jay, who'd been his other half for more than six years, who he'd loved so much it hurt sometimes. Losing Jay had been like losing a limb. Learning to live without him had been the hardest thing Paul had ever had to do. He still felt the shape of Jay's absence in his life every single day. His sexual self seemed to have died along with his lover. The desire he felt for Cory was shocking in its suddenness and intensity, and he didn't quite know what to do with it.

He leaned against the steering wheel and closed his eyes. "God, Jay," he whispered. "I wish you were here. I miss you."

Jay's gone, his reawakened libido reminded him, *but Cory's right here in town, and he wants you too.* He couldn't decide if his racing pulse was a result of fear, or desire. After a moment's debate, he pushed aside the urge to drive out to Uncle Charlie's Porch, and headed back toward home.

The looming storm burst over him before he even got out of town. Sheets of rain thundered down so hard he could barely see anything beyond the truck's hood. He almost ran into a shirtless figure in cutoffs and ragged sneakers, pushing a bicycle along the side of the road. It wasn't until he'd skidded to a halt and the drenched figure looked up at him that he recognized Cory.

He put the truck in park, reached over, and flung open the passenger side door. "Cory? Is that you?"

"Yeah." Cory peered at Paul from under a mass of dripping curls. "Paul?"

Paul managed to act casual, in spite of the way his hands shook all of a sudden. "Hi. Need some help?"

"Well, I could use a ride if it's not too much trouble. I'm late for work."

"It's no trouble at all. Here, let me help you get your bike in the truck."

He started to open his door. Cory held out a hand toward him. "No, that's okay. No need for you to get soaked too. I can get it."

Before Paul could protest, Cory shut the door. He had the bike stowed in the truck bed and was jumping into the cab within seconds, a tightly tied plastic bag in his hand.

"Thanks for this," Cory said as he buckled his seatbelt. "I really appreciate it."

"No problem." Paul glanced over at the soaking wet, half-naked man on the seat beside him before pulling back onto the road. "So what're you doing out riding your bike in the rain?"

Cory laughed, shaking his wet hair out of his eyes. "It wasn't raining when I left home this morning. I usually carry my poncho anyhow, just in case, but I had some stuff to take care of this morning and it took me longer than I thought it would, so I had to rush to get to work and I forgot my stupid poncho. At least I remembered to put my work clothes in a bag." He patted the plastic bag on the seat beside him.

Paul frowned. "So, do you ride on your lunch break or something?"

Cory stared blankly at him for a moment. Then understanding dawned in his eyes. Cory's cheeks went pink under his tan. "No. I, um, I don't have a car, I ride my bike to work. I work part-time at Willow Bend Outdoors, leading kayak tours to Otter Island. Had a lunchtime tour, and now I'm late for dinner shift at Charlie's 'cause I got a flat. I patched it, but it's not holding."

"Oh." Paul, sensing Cory's embarrassment, concentrated on watching the road through the pounding rain. What came out next surprised them both. "Listen, why don't I take your bike and get it fixed while you're at work? I can come back after your shift and drive you home."

"Really?"

"Yeah, really." Paul risked taking his eyes off the road for a second to smile at Cory. "What about it?"

Cory grinned, and Paul's heart lurched as he stared out the front window again. God, but the boy had a beautiful smile. Almost beautiful enough to make Paul forget the one quick glimpse he'd had of Cory's bare chest and long, tanned legs. Almost. The way the toned muscles moved under that golden skin caused a fierce ache in Paul's groin.

Paul shot another glance at Cory's face. Those green eyes were heavy, as if he knew what Paul had been thinking. *Of course he knows. You couldn't have been more obvious, idiot.*

"Okay," Cory said, his voice soft.

"Huh?" Paul glanced at the road to make sure he was still on it, then back at Cory. He felt thoroughly flustered.

"You getting my bike fixed. Driving me home. Yes, please." Cory looked down at the floorboard. "Normally I wouldn't ask, but I'm pretty much out of other options at this point."

"You didn't ask me, I asked you."

"However it happened, Paul, I'm glad it did. Thank you."

"You're welcome." Paul glanced over. Cory looked back up, giving him a little half smile from under a veil of dripping curls. Paul hurriedly turned his eyes back to the road again, squinting through the pelting rain.

The storm made the trip to the restaurant longer than it should've been. By the time they got there ten minutes later, Cory had found a relatively clean towel behind the seat and dried himself off as best he could. Paul tried hard not to stare at the rough cloth rubbing over that smooth skin, just the way his hands were itching to do.

"Let me off around back, if you don't mind," Cory said as Paul turned into the parking lot. "I don't wanna have to go through the dining room like this."

"Sure." Paul pulled the truck up as close as he could get to the back door. "What time are you off?"

"We close at nine, so I'm usually done by nine-thirty. Might be later if I got a customer who won't leave, but usually I'm out by then."

"Okay. I'll see you then."

"Okay." Cory turned in the seat and fixed Paul with a solemn look. "Thanks, Paul. I really appreciate this."

"No problem."

Cory leaned forward a little, those pretty lips parted like he was about to say something. Then he smiled, picked up the bag with his clothes in it and slipped out of the truck. Paul watched him until he disappeared inside.

🁫   🁫   🁫

"You're late, son." Joe, the manager, gave Cory a stern frown as he rushed in the door, shaking water out of his hair.

"Sorry," Cory panted. "My bike got a flat."

Joe grunted. "You have section four."

"Got it. Be right out."

Cory trotted into the bathroom, stripped off his wet shorts, and started pulling on his work clothes. They were a little wrinkled, but they'd have to do. No time to drag out the portable iron Alicia kept in her locker.

He thought about Paul while he dressed. That long, lean body, wrapped in paint-splattered jeans and T-shirt that looked like they'd been stomped in the dirt. The way that thick black hair hung in sweaty tendrils around his face. And those eyes. God, those eyes. Raking white hot over Cory's skin, making him want things he couldn't have, not right now. He stood gripping the edge of the sink until his burgeoning erection subsided, then headed out to earn his living.

⊞ ⊞ ⊞

Cory pocketed the meager tip old Mr. Jones left him and glanced at the clock. Quarter to nine. Forty-five more minutes until Paul came to get him. He shook his head, laughing at himself for acting like a high-school virgin.

"Cory!" Alicia nudged him with her elbow.

"Hm?" Cory didn't look up from the table he was clearing. He wondered idly what Paul would look like naked.

"You got a customer."

Cory sighed. "Now? Fifteen minutes 'til closing?"

"Yeah." Alicia grinned, brown eyes twinkling. "He asked for you special."

Cory started to say something thoroughly unprofessional. Then a thought struck him. His head snapped up, eyes searching the room. Paul smiled and waved at him from the little table in the corner. Cory smiled back.

"Here, I'll finish this." Alicia snatched the dirty glass he still held right out of his hand and popped him on the butt. "Go get him, stud."

Cory laughed. "Thanks, 'Licia."

She gave him a little shove and he strolled over to Paul's table, grinning like an idiot. "Hi, Paul. You're here early. Although it looks like I might actually be out early tonight."

"Yeah, the place is pretty empty, huh?"

"Sure is. Guess the storm's kept everyone at home."

"Guess so." Paul smiled that lethally gorgeous smile, and it was all Cory could do not to kiss him senseless right then and there.

Cory cleared his throat. "So, what can I get you?"

"Just a cup of coffee, if that's okay. I grabbed a sandwich in town earlier. Besides, I don't want to hold you up."

"Oh, you won't. I still have to do my share of cleaning up before I can go. Sure you won't have something to eat? Maybe some dessert to go with the coffee?"

Paul laughed. "Maybe I'll have a slice of that key lime pie."

"Coming right up." Cory grinned and hurried into the kitchen to fetch it, thinking that the pie wasn't the only thing coming up.

He kept watching Paul out of the corner of his eye while he cleared tables and swept the floor. Watching the way Paul's throat worked as he sipped his coffee, the devastatingly sexy way he licked the pie off his fork. Cory couldn't help picturing that wet, pink tongue sliding over skin instead of metal. He about came in his pants when Paul scooped a finger through the last bit of pie, stuck it in his mouth and sucked it clean.

When Cory came back from depositing Paul's cup and plate in the dishwasher, Paul was standing at the window, staring out into the dimness. Cory allowed himself a moment to admire the man's long legs and firm ass before announcing his presence.

"Okay, I'm set," he said.

Paul turned and smiled at him. "You were right about the pie. It's delicious."

"It is, isn't it?" Cory started toward the door. Paul fell into step beside him, limping just a little. "Hey, Paul?"

"Yeah?"

"Tell me if I'm being too nosy or anything, but is something wrong with your leg? It looks like it hurts you a little to walk on it."

Those pale eyes filled with sadness. "I was in a car wreck just over a year ago. Broke the left femur pretty bad right up near the hip joint. It still hurts sometimes."

Cory stared hard at Paul's profile, half-hidden behind a swatch of tangled hair. Something told Cory that worse had happened in the wreck than a broken leg.

"Rain's let up," he said as they stepped out the front door into a light drizzle.

Paul's smile said he welcomed the change of subject. "Yeah. Good thing, too. I never saw rain that hard in my life. Are all the storms that bad down here?"

"Not all, but enough of them."

"Damn."

"Yeah."

"Your bike's in the back," Paul said as they slid into the truck's cab. "June Horton down at the garage put a new inner tube on it."

"Cool. Thanks for doing that, Paul, seriously." He dug into his back pocket and pulled out a handful of bills. "What do I owe you?"

Paul gave him a surprised look. "Don't worry about it, Cory, it wasn't much."

"No, I can't let you pay for that. Now come on, how much?" Cory wouldn't meet Paul's eyes. He hated taking charity. Hated the pity in people's eyes when they gave him things he hadn't earned. He didn't want to see that look in Paul's eyes.

"Cory." Something in Paul's voice made Cory look at him. He was surprised to find no trace of pity in Paul's face. The only thing he saw there was a heat that left him breathless. "It's not a big deal, okay?"

"Okay," Cory said meekly.

"Good. Now, where am I going?"

Cory guided Paul to the dirt lane and the little run-down house at the end of it. His cheeks heated as Paul pulled up in front and stopped. The place looked old and shabby, and he wished Paul hadn't seen it.

"Thanks for the ride," Cory said, opening the door and hopping out. "And for getting my bike fixed. I'll pay you back sometime, whether you want me to or not."

"You can pay me back right now, if you want." Paul opened his door and met Cory at the back of the truck.

"Oh, okay. Sure." Cory started to dig the money out of his pocket again. Paul's hand covered his and he stopped, heart suddenly in his throat.

"I don't want your money." Paul's voice was soft and heavy. He stepped closer, so close Cory could feel his heat.

"Oh. Then, what...?" Cory looked up into Paul's eyes, and his breath ran out like he'd been punched.

Paul slid one hand into Cory's hair and the other around his back, pressing their bodies together. Cory let out a soft "oh" of surprise. Then Paul's mouth was on his, soft and warm, wet tongue urging his lips open, and all thought vanished in a rush of need. Cory wound both arms around Paul's waist, tilting his head to kiss Paul deep. The evidence of Paul's arousal slid against his own through two layers of cloth, sending electricity zinging up Cory's spine.

"Cory." His name emerged from Paul's throat rough and husky with desire. "Want you."

"Yeah. God."

Hands tangling together, they fumbled open buttons and zippers. After a few frantic seconds, their cocks pressed together, skin to skin, hot and dripping. Cory wrapped a hand around them both and pumped hard. Paul groaned. Cory felt strong, warm hands shoving his pants down past his hips, fingers brushing over his opening, and that was all it took. He came so hard his ears rang, mouth still locked to Paul's. Paul came a split second later, hips rolling against Cory's hand.

Cory leaned against Paul's chest, gasping for breath. "Wow."

"Yeah." Paul's voice was weak and stunned, his breathing harsh against Cory's ear.

Cory raised his head again, suddenly needing to see Paul's face. The pale eyes were heavy-lidded and sated. Cory lifted the hand that wasn't covered in semen and ran his fingers over Paul's swollen lips.

"I guess this is as good a time as any to ask you out?"

Paul laughed, stroking Cory's hair away from his face. "I guess it is, yeah."

Cory grinned. "Will you go out with me?"

"Sure." Paul cupped his cheek, gave him a light kiss. "What did you have in mind?"

"There's a big picnic and fireworks on the Fourth, out by the river. It's loads of fun."

"Sounds terrific. It's a date."

Cory smiled. "Great."

"So are you picking me up on your bike, or you want to take my truck?"

Cory was surprised into laughter. He got more than he could stand of the "Poor Cory" attitude from most people in town. It eased something inside him to know that Paul could tease him about a thing most people avoided mentioning.

Of course, Paul didn't know about Mama yet.

"Where do you live?" Cory asked, pushing away the thought of telling Paul the whole sob story.

"Not far from here, actually. Down at the end of Radcliff Road."

"Oh, did you buy the Thompsons' place?"

"Yeah."

Cory nodded. "Hell, you can see the fireworks from your back porch. The river runs not far behind your house, just before you get to that strip of trees."

Paul's hands slid up Cory's back, underneath his shirt. "Then come to my house and watch the fireworks there with me."

Cory ran his fingers along Paul's chest, wishing he could feel bare skin instead of fabric. "What about the picnic? Free food." He kissed Paul's throat.

"Mm. Well, how about we go to the picnic, then back to my house to, um..." Paul tilted Cory's chin up and kissed him. "To watch the fireworks."

"Oh. Okay. Yeah."

Paul's hand cupped Cory's head, and they kissed again, deeper this time. Cory could feel Paul's desire rising right along with his own, and felt utterly helpless to stop.

"Come home with me," Paul whispered against Cory's mouth. "Want to take you to bed."

The idea turned Cory's knees to jelly. But he couldn't, no matter how badly he wanted to. It would mean leaving Mama alone, and he couldn't do that.

"I...I can't," he gasped. "Have to... Oh..." Paul's insistent kisses, the demanding way his hands moved on Cory's skin, made it damn hard to think.

"What?" Paul dipped his head and sucked hard on Cory's neck, just below his ear.

"I... Mama. Can't leave her alone." Cory put both hands on Paul's chest, pushing them apart. "Can't. Sorry."

Paul's brows drew together. "Your mother sick?"

Cory nodded, cheeks heating. "I got somebody to look after her while I'm at work, but I'm it at night. She's in a coma, she can't be alone."

Paul stared. Cory waited, holding his breath. He didn't think he could stand it if Paul felt sorry for him.

"I understand," Paul said finally. His lips quirked into a wry smile. "Hell, I'd do the same for my mom if she needed it." He gave Cory a cautious look. "Would it be rude of me to ask what happened to her?"

"No. It's not a big secret or anything, everybody in town knows." Cory drew a deep breath. "She had a brain tumor, 'bout eight months ago. Doctor said it was a pretty bad one. They took it out, and she had radiation and all that. And she was okay, for a while. Then she started getting worse, having seizures and stuff, and they found out the tumor had come back. They couldn't take out the whole thing, but they got what they could and put in these special radiation implants for a few days to kill the rest of it. For a while she was getting better. But then she started getting worse again. The doctor said the radiation had killed some of her healthy brain tissue, and she wouldn't ever get back to her normal self. She's just kept going downhill since then. Last time she talked to me was more than a month ago."

Paul was silent for a moment, gazing solemnly at Cory. "Must be hard for you. Seeing your mother like that."

"Yeah. She was always so strong, you know?"

"What about your father? You haven't said anything about him, doesn't he help out?"

"I never knew him. Mama said he left when I was a baby. She wouldn't ever talk about him, and I learned pretty quick not to ask."

Paul's hands stroked Cory's back, over and over. "I should let you go. Let you get in to her."

"I guess." Cory didn't want to be let go. It felt good to be held.

Paul kissed him again, a soft lingering kiss that promised more to come, then pushed him gently away. He pulled off his T-shirt and used it to wipe the come off both of them. Cory tried not to notice the sculpted muscles of Paul's chest, the sprinkling of fine dark hair.

"Okay." Paul opened the back of the truck and hauled Cory's bike out while Cory put his clothes back together. "Guess I'll see you on the Fourth, huh?"

"Yeah. I'll come over to your place around three, is that okay?"

"Sure." They stood staring silently at each other for a minute. Then Paul reached out, folded Cory into his arms, and gave him a kiss that melted him from the inside out.

"Cory," Paul whispered, "I..." He pulled back, staring into Cory's eyes. His own radiated a hot desire, but Cory saw the fear behind it, and he wondered. Then Paul was gone, climbing behind the wheel of his truck and driving away before Cory could manage to say anything.

"Oh, man," Cory muttered under his breath. He was already halfway to hard again, just from the look in Paul's eyes.

He glanced down at his disheveled clothes, black pants splotched with semen, and just this once was glad Mrs. Harrison had left early.

◈   ◈   ◈

Paul drove home in a haze of need and confusion. The intensity of his attraction to Cory stunned him, made him want things he hadn't wanted since Jay died. He'd shocked himself, giving in so easily to the urges he'd honestly thought he'd never feel again. Wandering into his bedroom and stripping off his stained clothes, he still couldn't quite believe what he and Cory had done. Or that he'd come so close to taking the boy home with him.

He climbed into the shower and scrubbed clean before he could bring himself to look at Jay's picture. He picked up the eight-by-ten in its simple wooden frame and held it on his lap as he sat cross-legged on the bed. Jay smiled out of the picture at him, brown eyes shining, close-cropped blond hair setting off his sunburn. Wide shoulders, barrel chest covered with a curling reddish-blond pelt, muscular arms holding a tremendous salmon over his head. Jay had been so proud of that catch, his first in a weekend brimming with great catches. They'd celebrated by fucking right there in the boat.

Paul brushed reverent fingers over the photo. He'd picked that one to enlarge and frame because it captured Jay's essence perfectly. A big man with big appetites and a big heart to match, Jay had grabbed life by the balls, taking pleasure in every moment. Paul had always admired that about him. Even now, with Jay fourteen months in his grave, Paul could feel his lively spirit every time he looked at that picture.

"Miss you so much, Jay," Paul said softly, caressing Jay's image. "I didn't think I'd ever want anyone else. But Cory, he makes me... God, Jay, I want him so bad. I need to touch someone again. I need someone to touch me. And I wish it could be you, but it can't be."

He laughed bitterly. "And I don't know why I'm saying this to you, when you'd tell me to go for it. We always said that neither of us wanted the other to be alone if anything happened to one of us. And it happened to you, and I'm alone, and I know you don't want that. And I don't want it either. Not anymore."

So, what're you gonna do about it, Pauly? Paul could almost hear Jay's booming voice challenging him.

He smiled. "Gonna go for it, Jay-Jay," he said. "Gonna fucking go for it."

CHAPTER FOUR

Paul drove all the way to Savannah to buy condoms. It made him cringe to think of the unspoken questions he'd have to face if he bought them at Willow Bend's only drug store. So now here he stood, in the bland brightness of a big chain pharmacy on the outskirts of Savannah, feeling a bit foolish as he stared at the bewildering variety available to him.

He hadn't bought them in years. He almost didn't think of it. Then an offhand remark on the radio made him remember the first time he and Jay made love, how the latex taste had made him gag, how Jay had laughed until tears streamed down his face. Paul stopped right in the middle of mopping the kitchen floor to go get the necessary supplies before Cory got there. Because he was determined to need them.

"Flavored. Definitely." He plucked a box of mint flavored.

The memory of Cory's erection against his brought a rush of heat to his face. He glanced around, mortified by the bulge forming in his jeans, but there was no one to see. One at a time in the condom section seemed to be an unwritten rule. He grabbed a bottle of lube and hurried to the checkout counter. The gum-snapping young clerk rang him up and bagged his purchases without batting an eye, but he was still relieved to reach the privacy of his truck.

He glanced at his watch. Eleven-thirty. More than three hours until Cory was supposed to arrive. Plenty of time to finish the little bit of cleaning he had left and take a shower. He hummed along with the radio as he drove, pleased with himself for handling this so well. It wasn't until he'd parked the truck in the barn and headed back to the house that the reality of it hit him.

He was about to have his first date in over seven years, with someone other than Jay. And this date would most likely end in the bedroom.

He sat down in the middle of the kitchen floor, shaking. Squeezing his eyes shut, he tried desperately to summon Jay in his mind. He could still see Jay's smile clear as anything, could remember how he'd taken his coffee, all his little habits. But he couldn't quite recall Jay's taste, his scent, the feel of his skin, the sound of his laughter. Jay was fading from him, becoming a memory lovingly kept, but no longer sharp and immediate. The thought terrified him.

No use dwelling, Pauly, Jay's ghost admonished him, cheerful as ever. *Gotta move on. A life spent moping is no sort of life at all.*

Paul smiled, tears leaking down his cheeks. "Right, as usual, Jay-Jay."

He sat there and cried for a little while, letting himself feel the grief of losing Jay, mixed with the terror and excitement of starting something new. Crying felt good. Cleansing. When the tears trickled to a halt, Paul felt stronger. He pushed himself up off the floor and went to get ready for Cory.

▩ ▩ ▩

The rattle of bicycle wheels on gravel announced Cory's arrival a few minutes before three. Paul took a deep breath, smoothed his shirt, and walked out on the porch to greet him.

"Hi!" Cory swung himself gracefully off the bike before it had stopped and leaned it against the porch steps. His green gaze raked appreciatively down Paul's body. "You look hot."

Paul smiled. "Thanks. So do you." *That must be the understatement of the century.* Cory looked absolutely gorgeous in a tight white T-shirt and dark green cargo shorts that matched his eyes. His cheeks were flushed and his chestnut curls wildly windblown from the ride over.

Cory bounded up the steps. Paul had a moment of panic, wondering if it were okay to kiss him. He didn't have long to wonder. Cory walked up to him, buried both hands in his hair and pressed their mouths together. Paul sank right into it, pulling Cory close, running both palms over the curves of his ass as they kissed.

"Mm. Hi." Paul nipped Cory's bottom lip, smiling.

"Hi." Cory pressed even closer, kissed Paul's neck. "I've been looking forward to this all week."

"Me too. Come on inside." Paul pulled back, took both Cory's hands in his and tugged him toward the door.

They walked inside hand in hand. Cory grinned, eyes sparkling. "You know, last time I was in here I was ten. I was over here playing with the Thompsons' granddaughter, Jenny. Mrs. Thompson chased us out after we made worm soup in the kitchen."

Paul laughed. "I don't blame her. Worm soup?"

"We didn't eat it."

"You just used her good pots to make it in, huh?"

"Kind of." Cory squeezed Paul's hand. "How about giving me the tour? Just to refresh my memory."

"Sure." Paul swept his free hand in a wide arc. "This is the living room."

"Lovely."

"Thank you. And this," he continued as they strolled down the hallway, "is the hall."

"So it is."

"And here we have the kitchen."

"Very nice." Cory gave him a wicked smile. "No worm soup?"

"Fresh out, sorry." Paul pulled Cory into his arms, unable to resist. "Only two rooms left."

"Yeah." Cory molded himself to Paul's body, soft lips brushing his. "Let's skip the bathroom, huh?"

Paul swallowed. "Oh. Well, that only leaves—"

"I know," Cory interrupted. He ran his tongue slowly over Paul's lips. "Take me to bed, Paul."

Paul's breath caught. "Yes."

He led Cory into the bedroom. His heart thudded painfully against his ribcage and his hands shook. He glanced at the dresser, and his stomach dropped into his feet when he realized he'd forgotten to remove Jay's picture.

"Paul?" Cory laid both hands on Paul's cheeks. "Are you okay?"

"Yeah, I'll be fine." Paul managed a weak smile. "Sorry, it's just...it's been a while."

"Hey, it's okay if you don't want to."

"No, I do. I do. It's just..." Paul stopped, not knowing how to explain.

Cory followed Paul's gaze. He went still when he saw Jay's picture, then turned back to Paul, hurt stamped all over his face.

"Paul, who's he? Are you with somebody?"

Paul sighed. "Not anymore. Jay died over a year ago."

Cory's eyes went wide. "In that wreck."

"Yeah."

"God, Paul. I'm so sorry." Cory stroked his cheek. "Hey, why don't we head on over to the picnic, huh?"

"Probably should." Paul leaned his forehead against Cory's, fingers raking through the tangled curls. "Please tell me I haven't fucked this up already."

"Not hardly. We're coming back here to watch the fireworks, remember?" Cory pulled Paul's face to his and gave him a long, deep kiss. "I'm gonna get you in the sack before the night's out."

"Yeah," Paul whispered, lips brushing Cory's. "I think you will."

▦   ▦   ▦

Every year since before he could remember, Cory had attended Willow Bend's annual Fourth of July picnic and fireworks show. It had always been one of his favorite events of the year. Eating hot dogs and watermelon on the grass by the river, hanging out with his friends, watching the fireworks burst against a black velvet sky. But this year had a special shine to it. Being with Paul, seeing the sadness evaporate from him as they strolled hand in hand beside the slow rolling water, gave Cory a warm contentedness like he hadn't felt in months. It surprised him more than a little to realize how much he already cared about Paul's happiness.

As the sun began to sink in the West, Cory and Paul sat side by side on a little wooden pier on the river bank, watching the milling crowd and talking. Cory's head rested on Paul's shoulder, and Paul's arm was tucked around Cory's waist. Cory felt light and peaceful, his belly full of good food and his body tingling with Paul's nearness.

"What about her?" Paul asked, pointing to a tall, painfully thin woman, improbably outfitted in a sequined cocktail dress and heels. Cory had spent the last half hour telling Paul all about the residents of Willow Bend, and Paul seemed endlessly fascinated by them.

"That's Amanda LeBlanc. Now, anyway. Used to be Jean Cobb, 'til she went Hollywood and changed her name. She had a little part in some film or other last year, and now she can't get over the idea that she's a movie star."

Paul laughed out loud. "That's sort of sad."

51

"It is," Cory agreed. "I'd feel sorry for her if she didn't try to make everyone else feel lower than dirt all the time. But she does, so I don't."

"Makes sense." Paul tilted Cory's chin up and smiled at him. "Is there anybody in this town you don't have the scoop on?"

"Nope. I grew up here, remember? I know everybody."

"Now why do I find that unbearably sexy?"

"I don't know." Cory laughed. "That's kind of weird."

"You calling me weird?"

"I like weird."

"Oh. Good."

They sat silently for a moment, watching the crowd. A man in plaid golf shorts walked past, thick brows drawing together in a frown as he glanced at Cory's hand on Paul's thigh. Cory ignored him; Mr. Branson had always been one of the few bigots in town. Paul stared thoughtfully after the man as he walked away.

"Hey, Cory. Can I ask you something?"

"Sure." Cory twisted around to face him. "What?"

"Why is it that nobody here seems bothered by us?" He glanced at the retreating Mr. Branson. "Well, almost nobody."

"What do you mean, 'us'?" Cory asked, even though he already knew.

"I mean, you know..." Paul gestured at their joined hands, at Cory's leg where he'd slung it over Paul's. "Us."

"Us being gay, you mean?"

"Yeah. Not that I'm complaining," Paul leaned forward to lightly kiss Cory's lips, "because I'm not. It just seems strange, that's all."

"Why?"

Paul frowned, evidently thrown by the question. "I don't know. I guess I figured small towns weren't that tolerant."

Cory laughed. "Everybody thinks that, it seems like."

"So tell me why I'm wrong. Why's this place so perfect?"

"Truthfully?" Cory shrugged. "I don't know. Willow Bend's just always been like this, that's all. Mrs. Harrison says there used to be a commune here in the sixties, before the town started to grow. Maybe that's got something to do with it."

"Maybe."

Cory wound an arm around Paul's neck. "That's enough about Willow Bend. Kiss me."

Paul did, tongue exploring Cory's mouth like they had all night to do nothing but kiss each other. The unhurried sensuality of it started a hot glow low in Cory's belly. When they pulled apart, Cory saw his own need mirrored in Paul's eyes.

"Let's go back to the house," Cory whispered.

Paul nodded. "Yeah. I'd like that."

Cory stood, took Paul's hands and pulled him to his feet. Paul's arms went around him like they'd always belonged there. "Need you, Paul."

"Yeah." Paul kissed him again, hands running over his back. "I haven't wanted anyone like this in a long time. Not since..."

Paul fell silent, but his expression said it all. Cory nuzzled his cheek. "Then let's make it good."

Paul's smile warmed Cory right through. "I think it's gonna be really good."

They set off across the field toward Paul's house with their arms around each other. The rose-colored sunset and the fireflies blinking in the grass made Cory feel as if they were walking through a fairy tale. He turned his head and his eyes locked with Paul's. The hot anticipation there made his heart stutter.

Paul made Cory wait in the hall while he took Jay's picture and put it on the coffee table in the living room.

"Sorry," Paul said, blushing. "I just can't, not with Jay there."

"Don't apologize. I totally understand." Cory toed his sneakers off, went to Paul and wrapped both arms around his waist. "This must be hard for you."

"It is, a little. But not as hard as I thought it would be." Paul ran gentle fingers over Cory's lips. "It feels like this is supposed to happen."

"Maybe it is." Cory flicked his tongue out, tasting the remains of barbeque sauce on Paul's fingers. Paul let out a soft little sigh that made Cory ache inside. "God, Paul. Can't wait anymore. Please."

"Yeah. Yeah."

Paul took Cory's hand and pulled him into the bedroom, kicking off his sandals as he went. Before Cory quite knew what was happening, his T-shirt lay crumpled on the floor and Paul was tugging at his nipples, rolling them between his fingers.

"Oh, fuck!" Cory arched, gasping. He fumbled with Paul's buttons, trying to think past the waves of sensation. "Off," he demanded. "I need... Oh..."

His words degenerated into moans of pure pleasure as Paul deftly undid Cory's shorts and shoved his hands inside, cupping Cory's ass in his palms. He licked a long, wet line up Cory's throat and bit his earlobe. Cory shuddered when Paul pushed his shorts and underwear down to puddle at his feet and wrapped a strong hand around his cock.

"Cory," Paul breathed against his cheek. "Want you. Want to be in you."

The thought of Paul having him that way sent a surge of heat through Cory's body. He backed up, taking Paul with him, and they fell together onto the bed. Paul stared down at him for a second, pale blue eyes white-hot with need, then bent and gave him a kiss that nearly stopped his heart.

"Paul," Cory gasped between kisses. "I have...in my pocket, I, I brought..." Cory couldn't make the words come. But Paul seemed to understand. His lips curled into a knowing smile.

"Me too," Paul said, eyes sparkling.

Cory stared at him for a second, then burst out laughing. Paul joined him.

"Oh, man," Cory said when he caught his breath. "Guess we were both pretty sure, huh?"

"Guess so." Paul nudged a knee between his legs, and suddenly Cory didn't feel like laughing anymore. "Let me?"

"Yeah." Cory kicked his shorts and underwear off his ankles and opened his legs wide. "Fuck me."

Paul's eyelids fluttered, cheeks flushing pink. He stood, stripped his clothes off, and yanked open the drawer of the bedside table. Cory waited until Paul had what he needed then grabbed his wrist and pulled him down. Paul dropped the lube and condom on the mattress and wound his body around Cory's, pressing between his legs. Cory's skin tingled at the feel of Paul's erection rubbing against his.

Paul snatched up the bottle of lube and poured some in his hand. Cory moaned when he felt a slick finger nudging his hole, pushing inside. "Oh, oh yeah." He spread his legs wider as Paul slipped another finger in and began to work them in and out, twisting, stretching him. His body opened right up, even though it had been ages since he'd been with anyone. "Paul. In me. Now, please!"

"Yes. God, Cory." Paul kissed him, tongue quick and aggressive. He took the condom packet and pressed it into Cory's hand. "Put it on me."

Cory ripped the packet open with trembling fingers. He rolled the latex sheath slowly down Paul's prick with one hand, stroking the soft skin behind his balls with the other. Paul's eyes clouded.

"Paul. Now." Cory hooked a leg around Paul's back. "Need it."

"Yeah. Now."

Paul spread Cory open and penetrated him in one swift stroke. Cory cried out, that hot stretch piercing right through him. He wrapped his legs around Paul's waist, lifting up to meet his thrusts. Paul dug his knees into the mattress and plunged deep, arm muscles bulging as he balanced his weight on his hands.

Cory wanted it to last. He'd had wet dreams of having Paul inside him, fucking him deep and slow for hours. But his body wouldn't cooperate. He needed it hard and fast, and Paul gave it to him. They moved together in an increasingly fevered rhythm, their kisses hungry.

Cory gasped, writhing helplessly when Paul's cock hit his prostate. "Oh, oh Paul. Yes. So fucking good."

Paul stared down at him, eyes glazed and face dewed with sweat. "Cory. Uh. Gonna... Oh..."

Paul's eyes went wide, and he came with a sharp cry, his body shaking. His cock swelled, filling Cory so that he thought he might split in half. Paul leaned down and covered Cory's mouth with his own, hand reaching between them to stroke his shaft. Cory pushed frantically into Paul's hand. Paul's thumb rubbed over the head of his prick, probing gently at the slit, and that did it. He came hard, moaning into the kiss, both hands buried in Paul's hair. Paul collapsed on top of him, and they lay there panting for a while.

"Oh. Oh, wow." Paul eased out, pulled the condom off, and tossed it in the general direction of the little plastic trash can. He wiped his sticky hand on the bedspread then rolled onto his side, arms locked around Cory. "Jesus. That was just... Damn."

Cory snuggled against Paul's chest, one leg thrown across his thighs. "Yeah. I needed that. Been way too fucking long."

"For me too." Paul lifted Cory's chin and gave him a sweet, satisfied smile. "You're something else."

Cory smiled back, feeling relaxed and happy. "You good?"

"Never better." Paul slid a hand through Cory's hair, smoothing the damp, tangled curls out of his eyes. "So. How long can you stay?"

"I should probably leave by eleven, so Mrs. Harrison can get on home."

"Mrs. Harrison the lady who watches your mother?"

"Yeah. She's a retired nurse. She and Mama used to work together. Mama was a nurse's aide before she got sick." Cory ran a thumb across Paul's kiss-swollen lower lip. "Wish I could stay the night."

"Me too." Paul slipped a hand around the back of Cory's head and pulled him into a soft, slow kiss. He smiled when they pulled apart. "Mm. I like kissing you, Cory."

Something in that soft voice made Cory's heart race. "I like it too." He pressed closer, winding arms and legs around Paul's naked body. "Do it again."

Paul chuckled. "C'mere."

Paul's mouth was warm and wet and soft as a cloud. Cory felt like he could lose himself so easily in that wonderfully sensual kiss, in the heat of Paul's skin, the gentle but insistent way those elegant hands mapped his body. He ran both palms down Paul's back as they kissed, learning the feel of firm, lean muscles under silky skin.

As their kisses grew deeper, Paul's touch became more demanding, his fingers leaving trails of fire in their wake. Cory felt it might burn him alive. His hips moved, pushing his swelling cock against Paul's, searching for friction and finding it as Paul began to harden against him. He moaned, body aching with a need too large to contain.

Paul dipped his head and bit gently at Cory's neck. "Want to suck you," he whispered.

The thought of it tightened Cory's insides into a hot ball. He tried to answer, but his voice didn't seem to work anymore. He opened his legs and pushed on Paul's head, urging him downward.

Paul pulled away long enough to snatch another condom out of the drawer. He used his mouth to roll it over Cory's cock, so slowly that Cory was panting and desperate by the time he finished. Then Paul's mouth began to move on him, two fingers sliding inside him to nudge the sweet spot just so. Cory growled, clenched his fists in Paul's hair, and thrust down his throat. Paul took it all, his strangled moans vibrating up Cory's spine and into his brain.

It felt amazing, even through the thin latex. Heat and wet and suction, grasping fingers and a strong, stroking tongue. Cory tried to hold out, to savor the feel of Paul's mouth for as long as he could. But the sensation stirred something primitive in him, something that wanted only to be engulfed by the shattering pleasure of orgasm. He managed a few agonizing minutes, trembling on the edge all the while. Then Paul raised his eyes, their gazes locked, and the last thread of Cory's control snapped. His body bowed, arching off the bed as he came, mouth open in a silent scream.

He lay blinking up at the ceiling, all his muscles limp and heavy. When Paul's smiling face appeared above his, he reached up and pulled Paul down for a kiss. Paul tasted like mint with just a hint of bitter latex.

"Flavored, huh?" Cory chuckled.

"Yeah." Paul grinned. "If you can't have it bare, flavored's the next best thing."

Cory squirmed a hand between their bodies and folded it around Paul's shaft, stroking the head with his thumb. Paul's eyes went hot and hazy. "Christ, Cory."

"Sit up," Cory ordered. "Straddle me."

Paul pushed up and planted his knees on either side of Cory's hips. They stared at each other as Cory took Paul's cock firmly in his hand and started stroking hard. Paul let out one soft little sound after another, hips rolling, both hands digging into his inner thighs like he was trying to spread himself. Cory thought he could happily lose himself in the sight.

Paul was close enough that it didn't take long for Cory to bring him to the brink and push him over. He threw back his head and wailed when he came, thighs quivering as his semen spilled over Cory's hand and onto his chest.

Cory wanted to taste. Badly. He contented himself with sitting up and rubbing his face against Paul's prick, smearing himself with warm slippery wetness. His arms went around Paul's hips and he laid his flushed, sticky cheek against that flat belly. Paul's fingers combed through his hair. It felt surprisingly intimate, and Cory found himself wishing he could stay for more reasons than sex.

"Oh, man," Paul said after a few quiet minutes. "I can't believe I just got it up twice in less than an hour. That hasn't happened to me in ages."

Cory kissed Paul's hipbone and grinned up at him. "I know what you mean. Don't think I've ever done that before." He stroked a palm over the swell of Paul's buttocks. "It's nice."

Paul traced his fingers down Cory's cheek. The look in those blue eyes, tender and strangely possessive, sent a quick thrill through Cory's veins. "Wish I could paint you right now."

Cory's eyebrows went up. "You paint?"

"Yeah. Used to be pretty good, actually." Paul dropped down to sit cross-legged on the mattress, taking Cory with him. Cory pulled the condom off of himself, tossed it in the trash, then curled up with his head on Paul's thigh. "My stuff used to sell well back in Washington."

"Used to?" Cory took Paul's hand in his, lacing their fingers together.

"I haven't really painted anything since Jay died. Even after I'd recovered physically from the accident, nothing seemed worth doing for a long time. I was hoping that moving here would help me get past all that, provide some inspiration to do something besides wander around the house and wish things were different."

"And has it?"

"Yes, it has." Paul smiled, that sweet, slightly sad smile that Cory had already become addicted to. "You're the best inspiration there is."

"Oh." Cory smiled back, feeling light and a little giddy. "Good."

Paul bent down to kiss him. Cory wound his arms around Paul's neck and opened for him. The feel of Paul's tongue against his sent shivers over his skin. Part of him was a little frightened by how quickly Paul's kiss had become a necessary part of his life. But most of him didn't care that things seemed to be moving so fast, not as long as he could lie here in Paul's arms.

A loud boom from outside made them both jump. Cory opened his eyes just in time to see the darkness beyond the window light up green and gold. He laughed.

"Hey, the fireworks are starting! C'mon, let's go watch." Cory jumped off the bed, took Paul's hand and tugged.

"We're naked," Paul pointed out, grinning as he followed Cory down the hall to the kitchen.

"So? Nobody can see."

"I'll take your word for it."

They stepped onto the back porch. Voices drifted across the field, rising in harmonic approval every time another colorful explosion burst across the night sky. Snatching a towel off the top of the washing machine, Paul gently swabbed the semen off Cory's chest, then his own. Cory smiled at him.

"See?" he said, gesturing at the multi-colored lights. "Perfect view."

"It sure is." Paul dropped the towel on the floor, reached behind Cory, and grabbed his ass in both hands. "Hell of a view on this side, too," he added, moving a hand around to cup Cory's balls.

Cory pressed close. "You keep doing that, we're gonna miss the fireworks."

"The ones out there, maybe."

"They're awfully pretty." Cory leaned in and kissed Paul's throat.

"Not as pretty as you."

"Oh." Cory blushed under the weight of Paul's gaze. He felt suddenly shy, unsure of what to say or how to act in the face of such open admiration.

Paul chuckled low in his throat, pulled Cory tight against him, and sucked softly on his bottom lip. Cory's skin tingled. He was beginning to think maybe he didn't care so much about the fireworks after all.

Several minutes later, Paul broke the kiss. He nudged Cory's arm, and Cory turned around to lean against his chest. Paul's arms circled his waist, holding him in a warm embrace. Cory watched the fireworks through half-closed eyes, smiling to himself. He felt peaceful and content, and happier than he'd been in a long, long time. Just for a little while, he let all his worries fall away, let himself live in the moment without thinking about the future.

It was enough, for now.

✦ ✦ ✦

After the fireworks were over, they got dressed again and Paul drove Cory home. They took Cory's bike out of the truck bed, then leaned against the side of the truck kissing until Mrs. Harrison came to the door to see what was keeping them. Cory introduced them, blushing furiously at the teasing grin on the woman's face. Paul decided he liked her. She was sweet and polite, with a honey-thick accent and grandmotherly manner, but those sharp brown eyes didn't miss a thing. And she clearly doted on Cory, a feeling that Paul had begun to understand very well.

Mrs. Harrison invited Paul in, but he declined. He was horribly curious to see where Cory lived, where he ate and slept and showered, the place where he sat to read or watch TV. Everything about Cory fascinated him, made him want to know more. But Cory's expression said quite clearly that he would be ashamed for Paul to see. So he said he had to get home, kissed Cory one more time, waved to Mrs. Harrison, and headed back to his cottage.

He lay awake for a long time, staring up at the ceiling and thinking. About the evening, and about Cory. How effortless it was to talk to him, how well they seemed to mesh on every level. How good it felt to kiss him, to touch that smooth, tanned skin. How beautiful he looked caught up in the throes of passion. The memory of Cory rubbing his cheek like a cat against Paul's cock, semen sliding thick and white across his skin, made Paul ache. The boy was so responsive, so unselfconsciously sensual. Paul thought he could spend hours making Cory come over and over again, simply for the pleasure of watching his face and hearing those sweet little cries.

Having Cory in his life, and in his bed? That was something he could definitely get used to.

The idea didn't scare him nearly as much as it should have.

CHAPTER FIVE

"Cory? I'm here, honey, where are you?"

Cory half-turned and called out to Mrs. Harrison over his shoulder. "In Mama's room."

He leaned his elbows against the creaky old mattress and peered into Mama's face, frowning in concentration. He saw it again just as Mrs. Harrison shuffled into the room. A quick, fluttery twitch in Mama's left cheek, pulling up the corner of her mouth just a little and scrunching her eyelid.

"Baby, what you looking at so hard?" Mrs. Harrison asked as she came into view on the other side of the bed.

"Mama's face was twitching just now," Cory explained. "I think she might be having those little seizures again."

Mrs. Harrison pursed her lips thoughtfully. "Hm. Well, they'll be coming by this afternoon to draw her blood work for this week. They'll let us know if we need to up the dosage on her seizure medicine."

Cory nodded, absently stroking Mama's twitching cheek. Sometimes he wished that one of the nursing homes the Medicaid social worker had applied to could've taken her. She'd be well cared for. Maybe he could go to college then. He'd be able to afford it if he got a student loan and kept his job at Uncle Charlie's. And he'd finally have the time for a life. But every time the bitter thought crossed his mind, he shoved it guiltily away. Mama had raised him alone, working overtime every week to support him and make sure he had everything he needed. And she'd never once complained, never once been too tired to give him a smile, or a hug, or play a game of catch with him. He figured she deserved nothing less than that same devotion from him.

"Looks like rain." Mrs. Harrison peered out through the bedroom curtains at the gray sky. "Maybe they'll cancel your tour today."

Cory laughed. "Maybe. I'm not gonna count on it, though." He stood and stretched. "Speaking of which, I guess I should get going."

"All right, sugar. You be careful out there. Wind's kicking up, there's liable to be lots of waves."

"Don't worry, you know they won't send us out if the surf's too high. Oh, um, I fed Mama about an hour ago. She'll need to be turned in about thirty minutes." Cory gave his mother another worried glance. He bit his lip. "Maybe I should—"

"You should head on out," Mrs. Harrison insisted. "I've been looking after your mama for almost four months now, I know what she needs."

Cory gave her a sheepish grin. "Sorry. It just worries me when she has those seizures, you know?"

Mrs. Harrison's brown eyes softened. "I know. Don't worry, honey. Probably she just needs her medication adjusted a little. Wouldn't be the first time, probably won't be the last."

"Yeah. Okay, then. I'm off. Call the office if you need me, huh? They can reach me on the radio. And I'll check in before I go to Charlie's."

"That'll be fine. Bye, Cory."

"Bye. I'll be home around ten."

Mrs. Harrison was already fussing over Mama when Cory left, fluffing her pillows and combing her hair. He pushed the nagging worry firmly aside, jumped on his bike, and started pedaling toward Willow Bend Outdoors. And as usual, his thoughts turned to Paul.

It had been five days since the Fourth of July. Only five days since he and Paul had made love. It felt more like five years. Every time Cory closed his eyes, he saw Paul's face. He dreamed of Paul's lips on his, those slender fingers caressing his body. The memory started a hot ache between his legs.

A light drizzle began to fall before he reached Willow Bend Outdoors. By the time he parked his bike outside the office and hurried inside, the drizzle had become a gentle but steady rain.

"Tour's canceled," the secretary, Don, called before Cory could say anything.

"Yeah, I figured." Cory stood at the back window for a moment, watching the rain sweeping across St. Helena Sound. "Mind if I call home real quick?"

Don gestured silently toward the phone. Cory picked it up and dialed his home number.

"Hello?" Mrs. Harrison's soft drawl floated up through the receiver.

"Hi, it's Cory. Looks like you were right. They had to cancel the tour. So I guess I won't need you 'til around four."

"Hm. You seen your young man lately? Paul?"

Cory's cheeks heated. "Not since the Fourth, no. Why?"

"I like him. Your mama would like him too."

"Probably so." Cory swallowed the lump in his throat. "Okay, so. I'll head on back now, and—"

"You'll do no such thing. You never take any time for yourself, Cory. The Fourth was the only date you've had since your mama got sick. Now you got several hours free, and I want you to spend that time doing something fun."

"But...but I..."

"No arguments, now. I'm already here, my James is spending the day with his brother, and you know I don't mind a bit looking after Lorraine. Why don't you go visit Paul? I bet he'd love to see you."

Cory started to argue automatically. The thought of Paul stopped him. Paul's gentle voice and sweet, sad smile. His tender yet demanding touch. Those kisses that started soft and slow and ended in scorching heat.

"Okay," he said, his voice wavering with the lust he couldn't quite contain. "I think I will. Thanks, Mrs. Harrison."

"It's no trouble, honey. Tell Paul I said hello."

"I sure will. Bye."

"Goodbye."

Cory hung up and stood there for a minute, gazing out the window. Wondering why the thought of seeing

Paul again made his heart threaten to punch right through his ribcage. He'd been with lots of men before. He'd even had one more-or-less serious relationship, even though it hadn't lasted more than a few months. But nobody had ever made him feel like Paul did. A feeling he had no words for, swooping and fluttering in his belly.

"Everything all right at home?"

Cory shook himself out of his daze. Don was staring at him with a worried crease between his eyes.

"Everything's fine." Cory grinned, suddenly unable to contain the happiness welling up inside him. "Guess I'll head back out, since the tour's canceled."

"Okay. Watch yourself, it's coming down pretty hard."

"I will. See you tomorrow."

Don waved at him, and Cory stepped back outside. He laughed out loud as he straddled his bike and headed for the road to Paul's house. He didn't even bother with his poncho, since he figured he wouldn't be wearing his wet clothes for long.

That thought made him hot enough to evaporate the rain right off his skin.

🖾   🖾   🖾

Paul sighed as he dropped his pencil onto the little table beside his easel. He rubbed a hand across his forehead and glared at the half-finished landscape sketch in front of him.

"Dammit, it's just not right," he muttered.

He wished he could take the canvas and easel out back and paint the meadow from life instead of memory. But that wasn't going to happen today. The rain pattering gently against the barn roof seemed likely to hang around for a while instead of passing in the usual violent rush. Leaning back in his chair, he frowned at the canvas and tried once again to focus on the problem at hand.

He'd spent half the morning attempting to capture the peaceful beauty of the meadow behind his house. So far, it hadn't exactly turned out the way he wanted. Every time he tried to summon an image of the meadow, mental pictures of Cory kept getting in the way. Cory naked on his bed, legs up and apart, mouth open and eyes wide with orgasm. The thought made his jeans tighten.

Paul trailed his fingers over his crotch, feeling himself harden through the worn denim. He looked around before unzipping his jeans, even though he knew there was no one to see. He pulled his cock out, closed his fist around the shaft and began to stroke hard, imagining Cory's hand around him. His eyelids fluttered closed. He could almost feel Cory's soft, wet mouth sliding down over his prick, those callused fingers rolling his balls and teasing his hole.

"Cory..." His head lolled back, legs spreading as he stroked himself faster.

The sound of the barn door opening made him jump. He shoved his still-hard cock back into his jeans and zipped up, heart in his throat.

"Paul? You here?"

Cory. Paul laughed. "Up here, in the loft."

He walked over to the open trapdoor in the floor, a little awkwardly because of the way his erection pushed against his zipper. He looked down; Cory grinned up at him from the bottom of the ladder.

"Hey," Cory said as he started to climb up. "You weren't at the house, so I figured you'd be out here. Hope you don't mind me dropping by. My tour got canceled 'cause of the rain, so I thought I'd come see you."

"Course I don't mind." He shook his head at Cory's soaking-wet state as he stepped off the ladder. "Got caught again, huh?"

"Yep. But I don't care. If it wasn't raining I wouldn't be over here."

Cory peeled off his dripping T-shirt and draped it over the top of the ladder, then stepped out of his sandals. Paul reached out and pulled Cory into his arms. Cory's wet skin felt cool against his palms.

"I'm glad you came over, Cory." Paul gave him a gentle kiss, trying to resist the urge to throw him on the floor and ravish him.

"Mm. Me too." Cory's knee slipped between Paul's legs. He grinned and rubbed his thigh teasingly against Paul's crotch. "Did I interrupt something?"

"Um. I was just thinking about you, actually."

"Were you."

"Uh-huh."

Cory snaked a hand between Paul's legs. "And what were you doing while you were..." he leaned forward and ran his tongue over Paul's lips, "...thinking of me?"

Paul swallowed. "I was...uh..."

"Touching yourself?" Cory pressed closer, massaging Paul's erection through his jeans. "God, that's hot." He tugged Paul's zipper down and slipped his hand inside, green eyes going hot and hazy as his fingers wrapped around Paul's shaft. "Paul. Fuck me."

Paul tried to speak and couldn't. He buried one hand in Cory's hair, wound the other arm around his waist, and kissed him hard. Cory's mouth opened under his, tongue pushing in. The water from Cory's rain-soaked shorts seeped through Paul's jeans where their bodies pressed together, but he barely noticed. Nothing mattered anymore except the feel of Cory's body, the taste of his mouth.

He stumbled backward toward the threadbare old sofa under the window, pulling Cory with him. The backs of his knees hit the edge of the cushions and he fell half-on, half-off the sofa with Cory sprawled on top of him, one hand still clutched firmly around his dick.

Paul rolled over and pinned Cory with his body. He looked down at the man underneath him, at the tangled wet curls clinging to his neck and flushed cheeks, the golden skin gleaming with rain and sweat, and felt a strange stirring inside.

"God, Cory," he said softly, cupping Cory's cheek in his palm. "You are so fucking beautiful."

Cory blinked, long dark lashes brushing his cheeks. He reached a hand up to skate his fingertips across Paul's mouth. "Paul..."

Paul leaned down and they kissed again, gentler this time, slower. When Paul broke the kiss at last, he was surprised to discover that he held both of Cory's hands clasped in his, their fingers intertwined, arms stretched above Cory's head. His full weight rested on Cory's body, and those long legs were wound around his waist. It felt incredibly intimate.

"Paul, please," Cory whispered. "Need you in me."

"I... I don't... I don't have..." Paul squeezed his eyes shut for a second, fighting to make his brain focus. "The condoms, they're back at the house. I can't—"

"Don't care. Please." Cory sucked hard on Paul's lower lip, bucking his hips against Paul's.

"Um. But..."

Cory pushed at Paul's chest, forcing them far enough apart that they could look each other in the eye. "Paul, you...you were with Jay a long time, right? And there was nobody since."

It wasn't a question. Paul shook his head. "No. Nobody since Jay. I'm clean."

"Me too. Last guy I was with was almost a year ago. My last test was way after that, and it was clean." Cory stared up at him with somber, burning eyes. "Fuck me bare, Paul. Please."

Paul's breath caught in his chest. God, he wanted it. He wanted Cory's heat clenched tight around his bare cock. He leaned down again and captured Cory's mouth in a fierce kiss. "Stay there," he whispered against Cory's lips.

Paul extricated himself from Cory's grip, forced himself to his feet, and hurried across to his work table. He came back with a tube of lotion clutched in his hand.

He dropped it onto the sofa and stood staring down at Cory.

"Get undressed," Cory said, his voice low and rough.

Paul obeyed silently, watching Cory watch him as he yanked his T-shirt over his head and shimmied out of his jeans. Cory licked his lips when Paul pulled his underwear off, freeing his erection. "Bring that fucking hot cock down here."

Paul smiled. "Take your shorts off first." He grasped his shaft in one hand, stroking slowly.

Cory worked the wet shorts off and spread his legs wide, one slung over the back of the sofa and the other foot resting on the floor. The sight of that thick cock leaking pre-come on his belly made Paul's knees weak.

"Paul. God, please."

"Yes."

Paul knelt between Cory's legs and squeezed some of the lotion onto his fingers. Cory moaned when Paul's fingers slid inside him. His hips lifted, knees drawing up to open himself more, and suddenly Paul couldn't wait a second longer. He pulled his fingers out, grasped the backs of Cory's thighs in both hands, and buried his cock to the root in Cory's body.

Cory gasped, eyes wide and hot. "Oh! Oh fuck yeah, God, harder!"

"Yeah. Fuck. So good."

Paul let go of Cory's thighs. Supporting his weight on one hand, he took Cory's cock in his other hand and started stroking hard. The needy little sounds Cory made sank into Paul's brain, increasing his excitement to a fever pitch. He knew he wouldn't last long. It felt too damn good, the pleasure winding tighter inside him with every stroke.

Just as he felt himself about to topple over the edge, his eyes locked with Cory's. For the space of a heartbeat, time seemed to slow down. Then they moved at the same time, Cory reaching up and Paul leaning down, mouths meeting in a deep, almost violent kiss. Cory came in a warm wet rush, moaning, thighs shaking against Paul's ribs. Paul came a split second later.

They lay there for a while, kissing lazily. Cory's heart beat strong and steady against Paul's. Finally Paul broke the kiss, eased his softening cock out of Cory's body, and rested his cheek on Cory's chest. Cory's arms went around him, long fingers stroking his hair. He closed his eyes and breathed in Cory's scent, sweat and semen with a hint of the ocean. And suddenly he knew what he wanted to do.

Paul pushed up on one elbow and peered down into Cory's half-closed eyes. "Hey, Cory?"

"Hm?" Cory looked up at Paul with a dazed smile. "God, that was amazing."

"Sure was." Paul leaned down again and pressed a quick kiss to Cory's lips. "Do you mind if I take your picture?"

"My picture?" Cory laughed. "No, I don't mind. But why?"

"So I can paint you."

"Why do you need a picture for that?"

"Well, I guess I don't, as long as you're willing to stay right there until I'm done."

Cory looked thoughtful. "How long would that be?"

"Longer than you want to lie there, trust me. Probably a few days, depending on how much free time I have to work on it."

"Oh." Cory gave him a wry grin. "I see your point. Okay, so, how do you want me? Should I pose or something?"

Paul smiled, running his fingers through Cory's tangled curls. "No. You look perfect just the way you are. Don't move."

Cory's cheeks went pink, and something turned over in Paul's chest. He kissed Cory again to stop himself from saying things he couldn't possibly mean, then jumped up and went to the cabinet he'd bought to keep his supplies in. He loaded the Polaroid and started snapping pictures.

A couple of minutes later a dozen photos lay developing on the table. Paul picked one up and watched as the colors grew bright and sharp. It was a shot taken from between Cory's thighs, angled up the line of his body. Semen glistened on his flat belly and leaked from his open hole. Paul had to admit that he probably wouldn't need that one for painting purposes, but he hadn't been able to resist taking it.

He picked up another picture, a close-up of Cory's face. His swollen, softly parted lips and the sated gleam in his eyes made him look unbearably sensual. Paul traced his fingers over the picture. That strange, tight feeling tugged at his chest again. He shook it off and set the picture down.

"Got what you need?" Cory asked, smiling.

"Yeah, I think so." Paul plopped back down on the sofa, and Cory curled up against him, head resting on Paul's shoulder. Paul wrapped an arm around him and kissed his damp curls. "Thanks for letting me do this."

"No problem."

"So how long can you stay this time?"

"I have to work dinner shift at Charlie's." Cory drew idle patterns on Paul's bare chest with his finger. "Gotta be there at four-thirty."

"I'll drive you."

"You don't have to. I'm used to riding."

"I want to. And I'll pick you up after and drive you home, too."

Cory tensed against him. "Don't."

Paul frowned. "Why not? I don't mind. It's not any trouble."

"You just don't have to, that's all." Cory sat up and wrapped both arms around his knees. He wouldn't meet Paul's eyes. "I manage fine, you know. If I need help, I'll ask for it."

Suddenly it dawned on Paul what was bothering Cory. "Hey. Look at me."

Cory gave Paul a sideways look full of defiance. Paul laid a hand on his cheek, thumb caressing the corner of his mouth. "This isn't charity," Paul said. "I'm doing this because I want to be around you as much as I can, and hauling your hot ass to and from work gives me a great excuse to spend a little more time with you. Pathetic, huh?"

That got him a laugh. "We must both be pretty pathetic, then. Because I'd snatch any excuse to be with you too." Cory slid closer, throwing both legs across Paul's thighs. "Sorry. I get a little touchy about it all sometimes. I can't stand it when people give me that 'poor Cory' crap, you know?"

Paul slung an arm around Cory's shoulders. "I understand. After Jay died, even after I'd recovered physically, everyone I knew treated me like an invalid. Like I couldn't manage anything on my own. I guess they thought I was too emotionally fragile or something. I fucking hated it."

"Yeah. It sucks." Cory bit his lip, frowning, then suddenly took Paul's hand in both of his and pinned him with an intense stare. "Promise me you don't feel sorry for me, Paul. Promise me that's not what this is about."

Paul didn't hesitate. "It's not, I swear." He squeezed Cory's hands. "I hate that you and your mom are in this situation, but I don't feel sorry for you. I admire you, and I like you. That's all."

Cory gave him a wide grin. "That's all?"

Paul leaned close and brushed his lips against Cory's. "Maybe not quite."

"Oh yeah?" Cory kissed him, light and quick. "What else?"

"I want you," Paul breathed against Cory's mouth.

Another kiss, deeper, more heated. "Take me."

The first round had taken the sharp edge off their mutual need, so this time was slow and easy. They moved together in a lazy, rainy-day rhythm, trading gasps and kisses and soft little cries. It wasn't until after Paul's orgasm shuddered to a halt, seconds behind Cory's, that he realized he'd actually whispered the words that had taken shape in his mind as he came.

He held Cory, stroking his back and kissing his hair, and hoped he hadn't noticed. Because it couldn't be true. Not so soon. He chalked it up to heat-of-the-moment and pushed it firmly out of his mind.

🔲 🔲 🔲

Cory slipped in the back door of Uncle Charlie's Porch at exactly four-thirty. He clocked in, checked the assignment board, and headed for the servers' station. He thought of the breathtaking kiss he and Paul had shared in the truck when Paul dropped him off, and couldn't suppress a wide, happy smile.

"Hey, Cory!" Alicia said, glancing up from filling the salt and pepper shakers. Her eyes widened. "Whoa, what the hell have you been doing? Like I can't tell."

"Don't know what you're talking about, 'Licia." Cory gave her a wicked grin.

"You can't bullshit me, boy." Alicia finished screwing the lid on the last salt shaker and leaned against Cory's shoulder. "So, did you get that thoroughly fucked on your kayak tour, or did you play hooky?"

Cory laughed, not even caring that he sounded like a teenager with a crush. "They canceled the tour 'cause of the rain. So I went to visit Paul."

"Fourth of July guy, right?"

Cory's grin widened. "Yeah."

Alicia lifted Cory's hair and prodded at the bruise Paul had left on his neck during the shower they'd taken together. "Must be a real tiger in the sack."

"He is. Sometimes."

"And the other times?"

"The other times? He's so gentle." Cory shut his eyes, remembering. "He treats me like I'm something special."

"Wow. You've never been like this before."

Alicia's voice was unusually serious. Cory opened his eyes and looked hard at her. Her expression matched her voice. "Huh?"

"You should see yourself, Cory. You're practically floating." Alicia grabbed Cory's arm, brown eyes solemn. "How do you feel about Paul? Is this thing getting serious?"

Cory ran a nervous hand through his hair. "It's a little early to be getting serious, 'Licia."

"Yeah, I know. But it sure does sound to me like that's what's happening. On your end, anyhow."

Cory didn't know what to say to that, because it was uncomfortably close to the truth. He knew his feelings for Paul already ran deeper than simple physical attraction. He'd felt it happening ever since the first time Paul kissed him. Felt himself falling a little harder every day. Wanting things he couldn't have, because Paul clearly wasn't ready for that, in spite of what Cory thought he'd heard him whisper earlier.

Declarations made in the heat of passion were not to be trusted, and he wasn't about to build any hopes on this one.

"Cory?"

Cory blinked. Alicia was staring at him, concern written all over her face. She patted his cheek. "Be careful, huh?"

"Always am." He smiled at her, she smiled back, and they headed out to take care of the early diners who were already trickling in.

🔳   🔳   🔳

The night started out busy, and stayed busy until after closing. By the time Cory's last customers left and his work was done for the night, it was after ten o'clock. His irritation at the rowdy foursome who'd hung around for nearly an hour after closing vanished the second he saw Paul leaning against the side of the truck. Waiting for him.

Thinking about it later, he remembered only vaguely what they'd talked about on the short ride to Cory's house. A new movie they both wanted to see, the serial bank robber the police had finally caught in Savannah, the latest Willow Bend gossip. Only two things shone crystal clear in Cory's mind after he kissed Paul goodbye and headed into his house.

The first thing was that he was hard as a rock from Paul's kisses and desperately grateful that Mrs. Harrison wasn't there to see.

The second thing was that Paul had become absolutely necessary to him.

He tried not to think too hard about what that might mean. Paul was still recovering emotionally from a huge loss; he wasn't ready for a serious relationship yet. That being the case, Cory knew he might be setting himself up for a lot of pain later on. He knew he should probably back off a little, give both of them some time and space. But the thought of losing whatever it was that they had made him feel sick and lost.

He had a feeling it was too late anyway.

CHAPTER SIX

Cory figured that the thought of seeing Paul again was the only thing that got him through the next two weeks. *Two weeks and five days,* he amended, laughing at himself for counting the days. When he didn't have double shifts at Charlie's, he had breakfast and lunch shifts followed by the evening kayak tour. It made for long, grueling days, and he went home utterly exhausted every night. Watching the sunset blaze red and gold over St. Helena Sound in the evenings would've made it worthwhile, if only he had Paul there to share it with.

They'd had more than one quickie in the back of Paul's truck, parked under the trees near his house, but it wasn't nearly enough. Cory wanted so much more than a quick fuck. He wanted to spend time with Paul, talking and laughing and just being easy with each other.

He pulled his bike up to Willow Bend Outdoors late one Friday afternoon with a sense of relief. He had most of Saturday off, working only the dinner shift at Charlie's, and he and Paul had made plans for lunch at Paul's house. Not much of a date, Alicia had told him. But Cory didn't care that they weren't going out to a fancy place or doing something exciting. It didn't matter where they went, or what they did, as long as they were together. Mrs. Harrison had offered to watch his mother before he could bring himself to ask, but he still planned on paying her extra. If he could scrape it together, that is.

"Hey, Don," Cory said as he breezed into the office. "What sort of group we got tonight?"

"Big one. Twelve people."

Cory wrinkled his nose. "Crap. What're they like?"

"Not bad. Family of five, three couples, and one guy by himself." Don grinned. "He asked for your tour. Said he knew you."

"Yeah, well." Cory opened his locker and pulled out the yellow T-shirt with his name on it. "Pretty much everybody knows me."

"Haven't seen him around before, though. He said he was new in town."

Cory's chest went tight. He tugged his T-shirt on. "What's he look like?"

"Tall, black hair. Seemed nice."

Cory smiled to himself. "Paul."

"Hm?" Don looked up at him.

"Nothing." Cory shoved his waiter's uniform in his locker, slammed it shut, and spun the lock. "I better go. See you later."

"Yeah, see you."

Cory hurried out to the dock, heart thumping painfully against his ribs. What if he was wrong, what if it wasn't Paul, what if...

But it was. Paul stood a little apart from the rest of the group, eyes shining. He gave Cory a wide smile. "Hi, Cory. Surprise."

Cory flung himself into Paul's arms, laughing. "Hi yourself. Damn, it's great to see you."

He glanced around to make sure no one was watching before pressing a quick kiss to Paul's lips. Everyone in town knew he was gay, but making out with your lover in front of the customers was definitely against the rules, no matter what your sexual orientation was.

"So," Cory said as they linked hands and strolled toward the rest of the group, "felt like taking a kayak tour, huh?"

Paul shrugged. "Never done it before. Figured it might be fun." He gave Cory's hand a light squeeze. "Besides, I have kind of a thing for the guide."

Cory laughed, cheeks heating in spite of himself. "That's good, because the guide sure as hell has a thing for you."

Paul's eyes met his, and Cory's insides twisted. The look in those white-blue eyes made him feel hot all over. He leaned close, brushing his lips against Paul's ear. "You're riding in my boat."

🔲 🔲 🔲

Paul had booked the tour on a whim. For nearly three weeks, he hadn't seen Cory for more than a few minutes at a time. Waiting until the next day to spend some real time with Cory had seemed too much to ask of himself. So he'd called Willow Bend Outdoors and asked them to book him on Cory's tour that evening.

The tour proved to be even more enjoyable than Paul had anticipated. The kayak slipped silently through the calm waters of the sound, paced by a pair of playful dolphins. Cory steered their course with an expert hand, using his paddle as a rudder, while Paul and a middle-aged couple from Connecticut paddled according to Cory's instructions. The other two kayaks followed close behind, each with a Willow Bend Outdoors guide directing the customers in the art of paddling a kayak.

The trip out to Otter Island passed quickly. Before he knew it, Paul was jumping out into the warm, shallow water and helping Cory pull the boat up onto the sand. He stood with his hands on his hips, looking out over the uninhabited island. A huge white bird rose from the shore to his left, skimming across the sun-burnished water to the mainland. Paul took a deep breath of salty air, drinking in the peacefulness of the place.

"So what do you think?" Cory took Paul's hand, winding their fingers together. "Pretty, isn't it?"

"It's beautiful," Paul agreed. "I can see why you enjoy coming out here so much."

"Yeah. Always makes me feel good, even when I'm really tired."

Paul glanced sideways as Cory stifled a yawn. "Like now, you mean?"

Cory gave him a sheepish smile. "Been pretty busy lately."

"You work too much."

"I don't exactly have a choice."

Cory pulled his hand away and turned to haul the big cooler of drinks and sandwiches out of the kayak. Paul watched the muscles in his back working for a moment before laying a hand on his arm.

"I'm sorry," Paul said softly. "I didn't mean—"

"I know," Cory interrupted. "You're right, I do work too much. Sometimes it seems like more than I can do. But I really don't have any choice, Paul. Mama deserves everything I can give her. It wouldn't be right if I didn't do whatever I could to take care of her." He set the cooler on a big blanket that one of his coworkers had spread out on the beach, then turned back to Paul with a plea in his eyes. "Say you understand."

"I do." Paul touched Cory's cheek. "Just...just try to take care of yourself too, okay?"

Cory smiled. "I will. Now c'mon, let's get some food, huh? I'm starved."

The whole group settled onto three large beach blankets, laughing and talking as they ate. Paul found himself actually enjoying the company of the others in the group. He'd never been one to make friends easily, so the fact that he could have so much fun with a group of strangers came as a pleasant surprise.

After they'd polished off the sandwiches, chips and sodas, they began to prepare for a tour of the island. Cory whispered something to one of the other guides, a freckle-faced girl with two long blonde braids and a wide smile. Teena, Paul remembered. She nodded, grinned at Paul, and gathered the group of tourists around her. She was already talking about the sea turtle nests found on the island as she walked off down the beach, the tourists trailing behind her.

Cory turned to Paul with a wicked grin. "Okay, that's got rid of them."

Paul laughed as he pulled Cory behind a large sand dune. "Good."

"You don't want the island tour?" Cory pressed his body against Paul's, twisting Paul's hair between his fingers. "It's pretty cool."

"I'm sure it is." Paul slipped both arms around Cory's waist. "But this is better."

Paul bent to meet Cory's mouth with his. Cory opened to him, soft little sounds of pure want escaping him as they kissed. It felt like forever since Paul had been able to touch Cory like this, taking his time, holding him close and kissing him until they were both breathless.

"I'm so glad you came tonight," Cory whispered, planting little kisses on Paul's jaw.

"Me too." Paul flipped open the button of Cory's shorts and pulled the zipper down.

Cory's eyelids fluttered, his cheeks flushing as Paul's hand enfolded his cock and started stroking. "Oh... God, Paul. Feels good."

"Mm. Yeah." Paul nipped Cory's earlobe. "Love how your dick feels in my hand."

Cory's eyes went dark, brimming with a strangely tender expression. "Oh! Oh God, gonna come."

Paul tightened his fist around Cory's shaft, brushed his thumb over the head. "Come on, Cory," he said, his lips against Cory's. "Come for me."

A few more firm strokes and Cory came hard, clutching Paul's shoulders, his soft cry muffled by Paul's mouth. Paul slipped his hand inside Cory's shorts, cupping his balls as they kissed.

"I missed this," Cory murmured between kisses.

"Me too." Paul moved both hands up to gently caress Cory's face. "Missed having more than a few minutes a day to be with you."

Cory pulled back, green eyes heavy with something Paul couldn't quite define. Then before Paul knew what was happening, Cory dropped to his knees in the sand, fingers working Paul's zipper open. He shoved the shorts out of the way, grasped Paul's cock in one hand, and swallowed him down. The suddenness of it tore a harsh gasp from Paul's throat.

"Cory, God, yes..." Paul threaded his fingers through Cory's hair, fighting the urge to thrust.

As if reading his mind, Cory pulled back, gazing up at Paul with eyes full of lust. "Fuck my mouth."

Paul gulped. "I, I don't want...to hurt...you... Oh Christ..."

His words trailed off as Cory took him deep, throat muscles clenching around him. He tried to fight it. But when Cory wet a finger in his mouth and pushed it into Paul's ass, his control evaporated. Paul held Cory's head firmly by his hair, pounding into his mouth in short, quick strokes. Cory's finger massaging his gland sent shockwaves rippling through him. Before many minutes had passed, Paul felt the orgasm building inside him. He came with his cock buried to the hilt in Cory's throat. Cory swallowed, then sat back on his heels, grinning.

"Oh. Wow." Paul sank to the ground and wrapped Cory in his arms. "Jesus, Cory. The things you do to me."

"You taste so damn good, Paul." Cory slipped a hand behind Paul's head and gave him a semen-flavored kiss.

"Mmm." Paul licked a trickle of come from the corner of Cory's mouth. "So. How long do we have before everybody else gets back?"

Cory glanced at his watch. "'Bout half an hour. Wanna do it again?"

"Tempting." Paul shook his head when Cory yawned. "But I think somebody's too tired."

"I'm not all that tired," Cory protested. Paul gave him a skeptical look, and he grimaced. "Okay, so maybe I am. Like I said, I've been busy."

Paul rose to his knees to pull his shorts up and zip them, watching as Cory did the same. "Cory, please don't take this the wrong way, but...well, why don't you... I mean, your mom needs a lot of care, and you work so hard..." He trailed off, trying to find the right words.

"Why don't I put her in a nursing home, you mean?" Cory's eyes met Paul's. The heartache there, hiding behind the exhaustion, tugged at Paul's heart. "I tried, Paul. Couldn't get her in anywhere. There was a place in Savannah that had a bed and would take her, but it's too far for my bike, and I couldn't leave her there when I'd hardly ever be able to visit."

Paul took Cory's hand, stroking the work-roughened knuckles with his thumb. "You could keep trying. A bed might open up."

"Yeah. She's on a waiting list for the place in Hartsville."

"That's still kind of a long ride on a bike, Cory. What about that one right outside Willow Bend?"

Cory shook his head. "I went there first thing to check it out. It's a fucking pit. I'm not putting her there."

Paul sat gazing thoughtfully at Cory. An idea had begun to form in his mind. He wasn't sure how Cory would react, but he couldn't look at the dark smudges under Cory's eyes and keep it to himself. He took a deep breath.

"Cory?"

"Yeah?" Cory glanced at Paul, frowned, and looked harder. "What's wrong?"

"Nothing. I want to ask you something."

"What is it?" Cory touched a gentle finger to Paul's cheek. "You look so serious, Paul."

"Yeah. To tell you the truth, I don't think you're going to like it much. But I hope you'll at least listen to me, and realize why I'm asking."

Cory's face went blank. He pulled his hand away from Paul's. "Go on."

Paul fought the urge to take Cory in his arms and kiss him until that hard look went away. "Okay. Cory, I'd like to help you out. With your mother's care, that is."

Cory blinked. "What do you mean?"

"I'd like to pay for someone to stay with your mom all the time. In addition to Mrs. Harrison, I mean. She can't stay twenty-four hours a day, and your mom needs constant care. And I'd like to help you out with...whatever else you need as well." He'd almost mentioned the obvious need for major repairs on Cory's house, but the stormy look on Cory's face warned him against it.

"I told you, I manage fine." Cory stood and brushed sand from his legs. "I don't need your help."

"Cory, it's not like that. I just...I care about you, and I want to help."

Cory stared at him. Paul held his breath. After a moment, the hard glitter in Cory's eyes softened. "Sorry. Didn't mean to get all defensive. But I can't let you start giving me money."

"Why not?" Paul pushed to his feet and wrapped his arms around Cory's waist. "It's not charity. You know that. Why won't you let me help?"

"Because, it's just not right, that's all. I think..." Cory trailed off, chewing on his bottom lip. "I think we have something here, Paul. I'm not sure what it is exactly, but I like it, and I don't want to screw it up."

Paul plucked gently at the salt-damp curls brushing Cory's neck. "I like it too. Whatever it is. But I don't see how me helping you out here and there is going to mess anything up."

Cory cupped Paul's face in his hands. His eyes were solemn. "Money changes things. I don't want it to change us."

"It won't."

"How can you be so sure? We barely know each other outside the bedroom. I already know how to touch you, but I don't know your parents' names, or what you wanted to be when you were twelve, or even what your paintings look like. Whatever it is we have together, Paul, we don't know if it's strong enough to survive you helping to support me. And I need this, way more than I need your money."

Paul wanted to argue, to insist that the money wouldn't make any difference. But he couldn't. He'd seen firsthand how money could sour even the strongest relationship, and his relationship with Cory was still new and fragile, no matter how much he'd like to think otherwise. He didn't want Cory to come to depend on him financially, and to eventually resent that dependence.

He sighed. "Okay, I see your point. But keep it in mind, huh?"

Cory gave him wry smile. "How would you be able to afford a twenty-four/seven nurse anyhow? You rich or something?"

Paul's cheeks heated. "I have enough. Like I said before, my paintings sold really well back home. And there's other things." *Like Jay's money*, he thought, his chest going tight. Between Jay's life insurance and the money he'd left Paul in his will, Paul's already considerable bank account had more than doubled. "Rich" was uncomfortably close to the mark.

Cory's eyebrows went up. "Why do I get the feeling there's a story there someplace?"

"Because there is."

"Gonna tell me about it sometime?"

"I'd like to." Paul leaned down and kissed Cory's lips. "Gonna invite me in to your house sometime? I'd love to meet your mother."

Cory went still, fingers tightening in Paul's hair. Paul held him, and waited. "Yeah, okay. What about tomorrow? You can drive me home and come see her then."

"Sounds good."

"And maybe we can talk some more. You can tell me how you became fabulously wealthy."

Paul laughed. "Fabulously wealthy is overstating it a little, but yeah. We can talk about that."

"Good." Cory pressed a soft kiss to Paul's mouth. "C'mon, I'll show you some of the island."

"You changing the subject?"

Cory grinned over his shoulder as he tugged Paul toward the island's interior. "Yes. Might as well enjoy the rest of the evening, since tomorrow looks like being true-confessions day."

Paul didn't have an answer for that, because he had a feeling it was true.

⊞   ⊞   ⊞

Cory refused to let Paul drive him home that night. He wasn't sure why, exactly. He just needed a little time alone, to think. About the next day, and Paul, and Mama, and what Paul had said.

Part of him wanted to accept Paul's offer of help. The work never ended anymore. His days were spent at one or both of his jobs, or making repairs on the house. His nights were spent feeding Mama, giving her the medicines that kept her brain from swelling and kept the seizures at bay, turning and cleaning her. He snatched bits of sleep when he could, but it wasn't enough, and he knew it. He knew he couldn't keep going like this forever.

Paul had offered him a way out. And he'd turned it down.

The hell of it was, he couldn't decide whether he'd done the right thing or not. Despite what he'd told Paul, he did need the help. Badly. Mama's Medicaid paid for her meds and tube feeding, and the blood work that the home health nurse drew once a week, but that was all. The money to pay Mrs. Harrison came out of his own pocket. So did the money to repair the things he couldn't fix himself. Plus, he was still paying off part of Mama's hospital and doctor's bills. Having Paul pay for someone to look after Mama around the clock would free up enough money to get lots of things fixed that had been broken for a long time. Maybe he could get the car fixed, or even get another one. And there would be so much time. For lying in the sun, for reading, for sleeping through the night.

Time to spend with Paul.

"Dammit, Paul," Cory muttered as he leaned his bike against the wall of the house. "Why'd you have to be so fucking great?"

When he fell asleep in the chair beside Mama's bed, his head pillowed on his folded arms, he still hadn't decided whether or not to accept Paul's help.

Paul hadn't really expected Cory to accept his offer. He was determined to find a way to help, so Cory's refusal hadn't really bothered him. What set his insides churning was the look in those green eyes when Cory said he needed whatever it was they had together. Paul felt sure that he'd see the same look in his own eyes. Somewhere between his first sight of that wide smile and making love in his studio while the rain fell outside, Cory had become a part of his life.

And that terrified him.

"What am I gonna do?" Paul's fingers absently stroked the frame of Jay's picture. He stared into the deepening night from the front porch, rocking gently. "I'm not ready for this, Jay-Jay. I'm not ready to...to feel this way about somebody else."

You don't get to pick the time, Pauly. Jay's voice echoed through his mind, making his throat constrict. *When it happens, it happens. You just gotta hang on and see where it takes you.*

"I'm scared, Jay," Paul whispered. "Don't want to lose you."

Not gonna lose me, love. I'll always be a part of you.

Paul felt something hard and tight inside him loosen. He curled up in the rocking chair and closed his eyes. Within minutes, he was sound asleep, with Jay's picture pressed to his heart.

CHAPTER SEVEN

Saturday dawned clear and bright. Cory sat on the front step, sipping coffee and watching the rising sun tip the pines with gold. His eyes felt gritty with exhaustion. He'd woken several times during the night, imagining he'd heard Mama move, or make a noise. The result had been an endless night of worried wakefulness interspersed with short stretches of fragmented rest.

He yawned and dragged himself back into the house. He poured himself another cup of coffee and stood at the counter sipping it. In a few hours, he'd be with Paul. Just the thought of touching Paul, kissing and holding him, was enough to make Cory feel alive again. He smiled as he rinsed out his mug and headed into the bathroom for a shower.

🖼 🖼 🖼

Mrs. Harrison arrived around ten, just as he finished giving Mama her seizure medicine. "Hi!" he called when he heard the kitchen door open. "Let me get Mama turned and I'll be right out."

"Here, I'll help you." She appeared at the bedroom door a matter of seconds later, a smile on her face. "Well, doesn't your Mama look pretty this morning."

"I figured I'd go ahead and get her bathed so you wouldn't have to worry about it."

Mrs. Harrison gave him a sharp look as she and Cory turned Lorraine onto her side. "Baby, you know I'd have been glad to do that."

"Well, it's just that, you know, I'm not working until later today, this is extra time for you, and..."

"And you're feeling guilty for spending time with that young man of yours?" Mrs. Harrison clucked her tongue at him. "Honey, it makes me happy to see you taking some time for yourself for a change."

Cory's cheeks heated. "But it's still extra work for you."

Mrs. Harrison laughed. "It's not one bit of bother, honestly. Anyhow, my James is visiting his mama in Charleston this weekend, and I don't much like sitting around the house all by my lonesome."

"Like you ever sit around at all." Cory followed Mrs. Harrison back into the kitchen. "You're always doing something."

"So I might just as well do this." She took Cory firmly by the shoulders and steered him toward the door. "Get on with you, now. You have a nice time and tell Paul I said hi."

"I will." Cory stopped with the door half open, turned, and flung his arms around Mrs. Harrison's neck. "Thanks for everything. Really. I'd never make it without you."

She patted his back, then pulled away and laid a cool hand on his cheek. "Honey, I've known you from the minute you were born. I've watched you grow up into a fine young man. And your mama's a good friend. I'll always do what I can for you both." She gave him a gentle shove and shooed him out the door. "Now you go on!"

Cory smiled as he headed down the steps. "Okay. You've got Paul's number, right? In case you need me?"

"Right next to the phone."

"Okay. Bye, Mrs. Harrison. And thanks."

"You're most welcome, honey."

Cory watched Mrs. Harrison shut the door. He stood there for a minute gazing at the ramshackle house that had been his home for as long as he could remember. There were so many memories here. Happy memories, mostly. He and Mama had never had much, but they'd always had each other. It hurt to think of the time when Mama wouldn't be there anymore. And he knew that time was coming. He knew that what little strength Mama had left was rapidly failing. One day, probably sooner rather than later, Mama would die. He'd tried to prepare himself for that day, but he wasn't sure he was ready. He wasn't sure he'd ever be ready.

"I love you, Mama," he said softly. With one last look at the house, he straddled his bike and started pedaling toward Paul's.

🔳 🔳 🔳

Paul was in the kitchen when Cory arrived, cutting vegetables and singing along with the radio. The kitchen door stood open. Cory stood outside for a moment, listening to Paul's mellow voice, before rapping on the screen door to the back porch.

Paul glanced up and smiled when he saw Cory. "Hey, Cory, come on in."

Cory opened the door, crossed the porch in a couple of strides, and was swept into Paul's arms. "Hey, Paul. Mrs. Harrison says to tell you hi."

Paul laughed. "Well, hi to her too." He wound his fingers through Cory's curls and leaned down to brush their lips together. "This is just for you, though."

The kiss was soft and deep, spreading a feeling of warm contentment all through Cory's body. When they pulled apart, Cory laid his head on Paul's shoulder with a soft sigh.

"Mmm. This is nice," he murmured, turning his head to kiss Paul's neck.

"Yeah." Paul laid his cheek against Cory's hair. "Couldn't stop thinking about you last night."

Cory's heart turned over. He hugged Paul closer, hands sliding down to cup his ass. "Me too."

Paul lifted Cory's chin. "You look tired, Cory. Didn't you sleep?"

Cory gave him a little half smile. "Not much, no. Kept waking up, thinking I was hearing Mama move."

"How's she doing?"

"I don't know, Paul. There's nothing really different, but I just..." Cory stopped, trying to find the words. "It's just a feeling, but I can't help thinking that she's getting worse, you know?"

Paul cupped Cory's cheek, blue eyes brimming with worry. "Anything I can do?"

All the things he wanted and needed and wished for in the night flashed through Cory's mind. But he knew what was most important. He nuzzled Paul's cheek. "Just kiss me again."

Paul did, fingers combing through Cory's hair. Cory sank happily into it, concentrating on the feel of Paul's mouth on his, Paul's body in his arms. By the time they pulled apart, Cory's worry had evaporated, however temporarily.

"So what's on the menu?" Cory asked as he followed Paul into the kitchen.

"Nothing fancy." Paul took Cory's hand, lacing their fingers together. "Chicken, peppers, mushrooms and some potatoes. Figured we could grill. I have some fresh tomatoes too."

"Sounds great to me. Can I help?"

Paul smiled and kissed Cory's knuckles. "Sure. I'll get the chicken ready, you can finish cutting up the vegetables."

They spent a companionable time talking while they prepared the food for grilling. Cory loved it, loved the peacefulness he felt whenever he was with Paul. It felt good to laugh and joke and talk about nothing much. It seemed like he never got to be young and lighthearted anymore. Except with Paul.

One more reason to...well, to feel whatever it was he felt for Paul.

Cory wasn't exactly sure how it happened, but by the time they'd finished eating, the conversation had turned back to Mama. They sat in the lawn chairs Paul kept in his backyard, drinking beer while Cory told Paul his worries.

"I think maybe her seizures are coming back," Cory said. "I mean she's not having bad ones or anything, but I keep seeing her face twitching. Her med levels have been just right, though, so I don't know what's going on."

"Have you told the home health nurse?" Paul asked. "They might know what to do."

"Yeah. He called and told the doctor. She added another seizure medicine, but I'm not sure it's helping."

"Maybe it just takes a while to kick in."

"Maybe." Cory took a long swallow of beer. "It scares me, you know? Thinking about...about her dying."

Paul reached out and took Cory's hand, thumb rubbing his knuckles. "Yeah, I know. It can't be easy, watching her get worse every day."

"No, it's not. Sometimes I think it might be easier in the end if she'd just died of a heart attack or something. Something quick, you know, where she wouldn't be like she is now."

Paul's face clouded, and suddenly Cory realized what he'd said. "Shit, Paul, I'm sorry, I didn't think! Christ, what a stupid thing to say, I'm so sorry."

Paul gave him a sad little smile. "It's okay. Can't blame you. It's never easy to lose someone you love, no matter how it happens."

Cory stared into Paul's eyes. Before he could change his mind, he asked, "What was he like, Paul? Jay, I mean."

Paul dropped his gaze to the ground. "Don't ask me that, Cory."

"Why not? You loved him. He was a huge part of your life." Cory leaned against the arm of his chair, trying to read Paul's face. "Please, Paul. I'd really like to know."

Paul sat still and silent for several long seconds. Cory waited, Paul's hand clutched tightly in his. When Paul spoke, his voice was soft but calm.

"I met Jay on a rafting trip. It was my first time. Jay was an old pro at it. He stayed right there with me, kept telling me I was doing great even when we both knew I wasn't. After the trip was over, I managed to get up enough nerve to ask him if we could get together sometime." Paul laughed, the sound sad and full of memory. "I was still trying to play straight, you know, because we hadn't talked about that and I didn't know how he swung and I hadn't told him I was gay. But he had me figured out. He kissed me right there in the river. And that was it. I was a goner."

Paul fell silent. Cory kept still. After a moment, Paul began speaking again.

"He'd just moved to Spokane, and we found out we lived just a few miles apart. We started dating, and it just...it all just fell into place. For both of us. Sometimes it was like we shared one mind, you know?" Paul turned and met Cory's eyes. "I loved him so much. Sometimes it felt like I might not survive, it was so intense. I never knew I could feel like that."

"Sounds amazing," Cory said, a little wistfully.

The corner of Paul's mouth lifted in silent acknowledgment. "We built a house together about six months after we met. Jay had a couple of acres just outside town that he'd been planning to sell, but he decided to keep it for us. God, you should see the place, Cory. Trees and a stream and a split-rail fence. The house sits up on a hill. It's a log house, with windows everywhere. Jay always felt cooped up if he couldn't see out. He loved the outdoors. He loved life, more than anybody I've ever met." Paul closed his eyes. "It's so fucking unfair."

Cory lifted Paul's hand, kissed it and pressed it to his cheek. He ached for Paul, for all the pain he'd suffered from Jay's death. "Paul? Do you want to talk about the accident? I mean you don't have to, if it's too hard. But you know you can, right? You know I'll listen."

Paul turned to look at him again, blue eyes raw with something Cory couldn't quite define. "Jay had an irregular heartbeat. He had to take a blood thinner, to keep his blood from forming clots in his heart. That's what killed him. I was driving, Cory. The drunk driver hit my side of the car. But Jay's head hit the passenger-side window, and because of that fucking blood thinner he bled into his brain. They couldn't save him. They got him out of the car and to the hospital within probably twenty minutes, but the brain damage was so massive that there was nothing they could do. It took them more than an hour to extract me from the car, and by the time I got to the hospital he was dead. Didn't even know it until later, because they took me straight to surgery, and then I was sedated and on a ventilator for five days. By the time I woke up, his parents had already buried him. I never even got to say goodbye, or tell him I loved him."

Cory swallowed the lump in his throat. "I'm sure he knew, Paul."

"I know. But it's not the same." Paul drew a shaking breath. "He shouldn't have died, Cory."

Cory didn't know quite what to say to that. He stared at the trees in the distance, trying to squelch the jealousy he couldn't help feeling. *Of course Paul feels that way,* he told himself. *Jay was his partner for years. They loved each other. You can't just turn off a feeling that strong.*

The question in the back of his mind that wouldn't go away was, would Paul ever be able to truly let Jay go and move on?

"Hey." Paul's soft voice at his side brought Cory out of his thoughts. Their eyes met. Paul's expression was very serious. "I'll always love him, Cory. And it's hard to let him go. But I'm trying. I really am." Paul scooted to the edge of his chair, leaned forward, and gently touched Cory's cheek. "Be patient with me, huh? I think this, whatever we've got going here, is worth hanging onto."

"Yeah. So do I." Cory smiled as Paul's long fingers traced the line of his jaw. "I know this can't be easy for you, Paul. It's okay. I'll be here."

Paul's smile made the afternoon sun seem dim. He pulled Cory to him, leaning their foreheads together. "Thank you."

Like I have any choice, Cory thought as Paul cupped his face in both hands and kissed him. The need rose inside him like it always did as the kiss deepened and Paul's hands wandered lower. *Like I could do anything else but be there for you.*

He didn't say it. He figured Paul had enough of a burden to carry without knowing how hard he'd already fallen.

⊞　⊞　⊞

He'd sort of hoped Paul would forget about coming in to meet Mama. The idea of Paul seeing exactly how poor he was made him cringe inside, especially after hearing about Paul and Jay's beautiful home. And he felt oddly shy about bringing Paul to Mama. He wasn't sure why. He knew Mama would've liked him.

Maybe because Mama was dying by inches, slipping a little further into the past with every passing day. And Paul just might be his future.

He should've known Paul wouldn't forget.

"Aren't you going to invite me in?" Paul asked, his voice carefully casual.

They sat in front of Cory's house, in the cab of Paul's truck. Paul had insisted on driving Cory to work, then picking him up and driving him home again afterward. It was now nearly ten p.m., the fierce heat of the day had dissipated, and the cool night air buzzed with the songs of bullfrogs and crickets. Cory felt he would be perfectly happy to sit right there all night. But he knew he couldn't. Paul had laid himself open for Cory. Cory figured he owed Paul nothing less.

"Yeah, okay," he said. "But don't expect too much. We've lived here ever since I was a baby, and the house was already old when Mama bought it, and I can't always get everything fixed. Mrs. Harrison does lots of housework for me even though I keep telling her she doesn't have to, so at least it's pretty clean, but—"

"Cory. Don't worry so much about how the house might look. That doesn't matter to me. The reason I'm here is because this is your home, and I want to see where you live. And I really want to meet the mother of the guy I'm..." Paul stopped, bit his lip. "The guy I'm dating. Okay?"

"Okay," Cory said, trying to ignore the way his pulse was racing suddenly. "C'mon."

Paul took his hand as they climbed the three sagging steps to the kitchen door and went inside. The pressure of Paul's fingers wound through his made him feel just a little stronger.

"Mrs. Harrison?" Cory called. "I'm home. Paul's here, he wants to meet Mama."

Mrs. Harrison appeared through the doorway to the living room, beaming. "Why, Paul, it's so nice to see you!"

Paul smiled. "It's good to see you, too, Mrs. Harrison."

"Would you like something to drink?"

"No, thank you. I can't stay long. I just..." Paul stopped, glanced at Cory and squeezed his hand. "I thought it was time I met Cory's mother."

Mrs. Harrison turned and headed toward the short hallway on the other side of the living room, motioning Paul and Cory to follow. "You'll have to come back to Lorraine's bedroom, I'm afraid. She's not able to get up and about."

"She can't talk to you either," Cory added. "We don't know if she can hear anything, or understand anything, but we talk to her anyhow. Just in case." Cory figured Mama wasn't really aware of anything anymore, though they tried to pretend she was. The knowledge made him feel hollow inside.

Paul kept Cory's hand firmly in his as they all trooped into the bedroom. Cory gave him a grateful smile.

"Paul, this is my mom, Lorraine." Cory stepped over to the bed, bent and kissed his mother's brow. "Mama, this is the guy I was telling you about. This is Paul Gordon."

Cory straightened up again, watching Paul closely. Waiting to see how Paul would react.

Paul stepped forward and took Mama's hand without letting go of Cory's. "Mrs. Saunders, I'm so happy to meet you." He glanced at Cory. "You have a wonderful son."

Cory's chest tightened. He smiled, and knew it looked sappy as hell, but he couldn't seem to help it. That was just how Paul made him feel.

Mrs. Harrison patted Paul's arm. "Paul, I'm happy you came to meet Lorraine. I wish you could've met her when she was well."

"Me too," Paul said. "On both counts."

"Why don't you boys go sit down while I give Lorraine her medicines?" Mrs. Harrison opened the drawer of the bedside table and took out prescription bottles and a pill crusher. "I made some mint tea earlier, Cory, it's in the refrigerator. Go pour yourselves some. I'll be out in a minute."

Cory started to protest that he could give Mama her meds. Paul spoke up before he could say anything.

"That would be fine, Mrs. Harrison." Paul tugged Cory toward the door. "Come on, let's have some of that tea."

Cory trailed after Paul, glancing over his shoulder as they left Mama's room. He took the pitcher of cold mint tea out of the refrigerator and filled two large plastic tumblers. He could feel Paul's eyes on him.

Paul took the cup Cory handed him. "Thanks."

"Sure."

Silence. They sat down at the table. Cory took a sip of tea. He kept his gaze resolutely on the table top, picking idly at a chip in the faded blue Formica.

"Cory?"

"Hm?"

"Look at me."

Cory looked up reluctantly. Paul's gaze was fixed intently on his face.

"I'm sorry, Cory," Paul said, his voice soft. "I didn't mean to push you into this before you were ready."

Cory shook his head. "No, you didn't push me. I wanted you to meet Mama. I don't know why I feel like this."

"Like what?" Paul reached across the table and took Cory's hand. "Tell me."

"Like I just cut myself open. Like I'm naked in front of a crowd." Cory closed his eyes, trying to find the right words. "I can't explain it, Paul."

"It's okay. I think I know. You just shared something with me that you don't share with anyone, other than Mrs. Harrison, and that makes you feel vulnerable."

Cory let out a soft laugh. "Yeah, I guess so." He opened his eyes again and gave Paul a wry smile. "Pathetic, huh?"

"No. Not at all." Paul pressed a light kiss to Cory's knuckles. "You can trust me with this, Cory. I hope you know that."

The odd ache in Cory's chest eased. Paul had come face to face with the reality of his poverty and Mama's illness, and it hadn't changed how Paul looked at him at all. That simple fact lifted a weight Cory hadn't even realized he was carrying. He smiled.

"I know. Thank you." Cory leaned across the table. "Kiss me?"

Paul smiled, leaned forward and met Cory's mouth with his. The kiss was soft and tender, soothing Cory like nothing else could. He slipped a hand around the back of Paul's neck, coiling soft strands of hair around his fingers as they kissed.

They drew reluctantly apart when they heard Mrs. Harrison's footsteps. She smiled at them, eyes twinkling. "Cory, your mama's all set for a while. I'm heading home now. Nice to see you again, Paul. You take care."

"I will." Paul stood to shake Mrs. Harrison's hand. "You do the same."

"Bye," Cory said. "See you tomorrow."

"Bye, honey." She patted Cory's shoulder. "I'll be here at ten. You try and get some sleep, you hear? You can't keep going like you are without a good night's rest now and then."

Cory didn't answer. Paul frowned as the screen door swung shut behind Mrs. Harrison. "Cory? You haven't been sleeping? It wasn't just last night?"

Cory shrugged. "Mama needs turning every two hours, and she needs meds at midnight and four. Who else is gonna do it but me?"

Paul leaned on his elbows, giving Cory a concerned look. "Let me help, Cory. Let me at least pay someone to stay at night."

Cory felt his throat constrict. "Paul, don't."

"Can't you at least think about it?"

"I don't want your money."

"Why?"

"You know why."

Paul took both of Cory's hands in his. "I understand why you think it'll change us. But it doesn't have to. We won't let it."

Cory pulled his hands away and stood up, turning his back to Paul. He didn't want Paul to see the sudden anger that rose inside him. He couldn't find the words to express precisely how he felt. He was torn between his undeniable need for help and the certainty that if he accepted Paul's offer, it would build a wall between them.

It wasn't so much the debt he'd owe Paul that bothered him. It was the fear of becoming nothing but a charity project. He'd begun to hope for much more than that, and it made him furious that Paul couldn't see.

He started when he felt Paul's hands on his shoulders, but didn't move. "Don't be angry, Cory."

Cory leaned back against Paul's chest. Paul slipped both arms around him, and he felt a little calmer. "I'm not mad. Well, not mad at you, anyhow. I just don't want to be your pet charity."

He felt Paul tense against him. "Is that how you see me? Is that what you think I want?"

Cory was silent for a moment. "I don't want to think that," he answered finally, his voice barely above a whisper.

Paul turned Cory to face him. "You could never be a charity case to me. I care about you, Cory. It kills me to see you pushing yourself so hard." Paul palmed Cory's cheek, fingers brushing the dark smudges under his eye. "I just want to help."

Cory leaned his head against Paul's shoulder, as much to avoid that sharp blue gaze as anything. "You never told me how you got to be rich."

Paul sighed, but didn't fight the change of subject. "I made a pretty comfortable living as an artist, mostly from commissioned works for businesses. You couldn't have called me rich by any means, but I was able to support myself with it at least. Jay was rich, though. He'd made a lot on real-estate investment. It always surprised people to find out how sharp Jay was when it came to business, because he was such a good person. He was..." Paul stopped, took a deep breath, and started again. "He was the most generous person I ever knew."

Cory wrapped his arms around Paul's waist. "You don't have to tell me."

"No, I want to." Paul pressed his cheek against Cory's hair. "Jay was worth about twelve million when he...when he died. His will divided half of it between several of his favorite children's charities, and left the rest to me. And he'd made me the beneficiary of his life-insurance policy as well. I didn't know he'd done that. He never told me. I can't even explain how I felt when I found out."

"I can imagine." Cory lifted his head to meet Paul's gaze. The pale eyes were full of sorrow. "It must've been hard."

"It was. At first, I wouldn't take any of what he'd left me. I couldn't stand the thought of benefitting financially from Jay's death. Then my mom sat me down and told me to look at it from Jay's point of view. That Jay loved me and wanted to look after me, and I should try to see the money for what it was. Jay's final gift to me." Paul's lips curved into a sad little smile. "She was right, of course. I would've done the same for Jay. Matter of fact, if I had died instead of him, he would've gotten everything I had. It wouldn't have been nearly as much, but it would've been his."

"So you took the money?"

"Yeah. I gave most of the insurance money to the local children's hospital. Jay would've liked that. He loved kids. But I kept the money from his will. Every dime. I used some of it to move here. Selfish of me, I know. But I had to. I couldn't stay there, not without Jay."

"You weren't selfish." Cory reached up and cradled Paul's face in his hands. "I'm glad you moved here, Paul. I'm sorry Jay died, but I'm glad you're here. Does that make *me* selfish?"

Paul smiled. "No. I don't think it does."

As they kissed again, Cory wondered if Paul would still say that if he could see inside Cory's head right then. *I am selfish,* Cory thought. *Because I'm glad that I have this now, even though Jay had to die for it to happen.* He clutched Paul tighter against him, as if his need could somehow bind them permanently together.

They didn't make love. Partly because of having already had two rounds earlier at Paul's. But mostly because Cory felt horribly uncomfortable with the thought of having sex in this house. He couldn't have explained why if his life depended on it, but Paul seemed to understand. He gave Cory a sweet, lingering kiss and left with the promise to call him the next day.

After Paul had gone, Cory sat at the kitchen table, absently sipping his tea and thinking. About Paul, and whatever they were becoming to each other. Cory could feel the bond between them deepen every time they touched, or kissed, or made love. Paul's presence in his life gave him a sense of stability that he hadn't felt in a long time. Not since the day Mama came home from the doctor's office and told him those headaches she'd been having were caused by a massive brain tumor.

Part of him desperately wanted to let Paul help him. He was constantly tired lately, mind and body leaden from overwork and sleep deprivation. And he couldn't deny that Mama would probably benefit from the extra help. But his gut told him that if he accepted what Paul was offering him, it would mean the death of something he'd come to need far more than money. He couldn't let that happen, no matter what.

"I can do this," he declared to the empty kitchen. "I don't need any help. I'm fine."

Sitting there at the worn and stained table and struggling to keep his eyes open, Cory wondered who he was trying to convince.

CHAPTER EIGHT

Paul continued to offer his help over the next several days. He tried not to mind that Cory kept saying no. He understood Cory's reasons, even though he didn't agree with them. Only when Cory's refusal became harsh did Paul stop offering.

They saw each other almost every day, though Cory's busy schedule didn't allow for anything more than short conversations or a few stolen kisses. It felt to Paul like years since the last time he'd had Cory's bare body in his arms. He'd even begun to dream about sex with Cory. Dreams that woke him gasping in the night, wet and sticky and shaking. The fact that he'd had the reality just made the nocturnal fantasies harder to deal with.

Paul lasted exactly ten days before the escalating dreams and a nearly constant physical need drove him to contemplate a drastic course of action.

"This has got to stop," Paul mumbled to himself as he sat slumped over the kitchen table, hollow-eyed from lack of sleep after a particularly erotic dream. Part of him felt a little guilty for wanting Cory so badly that it dominated not only his dreams, but his every waking thought. In some ways, it still felt like a betrayal of his love for Jay. But in his heart, he knew he'd never betrayed Jay. He knew that Jay would always be a part of him, and that he would've been happy to see him move on with his life.

Paul was dressed and climbing into his truck before he'd consciously acknowledged his decision. He had to laugh at himself as he pulled out of the driveway and started toward Cory's house. Although he'd never said it out loud, Cory was hesitant about having Paul show up unexpectedly at his house, and Paul knew it. He knew he was risking making Cory angry, but the aching need inside him overshadowed everything else.

No one answered the door when Paul knocked. He had a moment of frustration, thinking Cory had left for work already. Then he saw Cory's battered bike leaning against the house and figured he must be around back.

Sure enough, when Paul rounded the corner of the house, he spotted Cory immediately, hanging laundry out on a line strung between two sturdy oak trees. Paul stood silently for a moment, just watching. Watching the sweat roll down Cory's bare back to soak into the waistband of his tattered cutoffs. Watching his muscles flex as he slung a large, wet sheet over the line. Heat pooled in Paul's groin.

A few quick strides put Paul close enough to smell Cory's skin. He touched one tanned shoulder. Cory spun around. Paul had one endless second to watch his eyes shade from fear to surprise to desire. Then they were in each other's arms, pulling each other to the ground. Kissing without finesse, open-mouthed, hard and hungry, fingers grasping and bruising as clothes were torn off and discarded.

"Shouldn't do this," Cory gasped against Paul's mouth. "Not here. Mama."

Paul rolled and pinned Cory to the ground. Lodged between Cory's open legs, he ground their erections together. Cory moaned, cheeks flushing.

"It'll be okay," Paul promised. He leaned down and bit Cory's chin. "Come on. I need it. *You* need it."

Cory didn't deny it. He grabbed Paul's hair in both hands and kissed him hard. "I want it from behind."

Paul's breath hitched. He pushed himself up onto his knees. "Turn over."

Cory scrambled to obey. Paul thought he could come just from the sight of Cory like that, on knees and elbows on the ground, thighs spread and ass in the air. Bits of grass clung to his skin and hair. Paul leaned over, molding himself to Cory's back.

"There's lube in my pocket," he whispered, and flicked his tongue into Cory's ear. "Hand it to me?"

Cory lunged for Paul's shorts, which lay inside out about a foot from his right hand. He fumbled for the little bottle and handed it to Paul. "Hurry."

"Yeah." Paul squeezed lube onto his fingers. He let the bottle drop to the ground and slid a finger into Cory's hole.

Cory sucked in a sharp breath. "Oh, fuck, fuck yes, Paul, more!"

Paul added a second finger, twisting them to brush Cory's gland. Cory whimpered, muscles clenching around Paul's fingers. Paul closed his eyes.

"God, Cory, can't wait."

"Yeah. Fuck me."

Paul sat up on his knees, spread Cory open, and shoved his cock in. Cory keened and clawed the grass, his thighs shaking against Paul's. The sight and sound and feel of Cory coming undone was all it took to snap Paul's tenuous control. He got a firm hold on Cory's hipbones and started pounding into him.

It was hard and rough and over too quickly. Everything went blank and silent with the intensity of Paul's orgasm. When the world came back, his hand was around Cory's prick, pumping hard. Cory gasped, shuddered, and came, his body undulating around Paul's cock.

Not quite the slow, sweet lovemaking Paul really wanted, but enough to dull the craving, for a little while.

Paul pulled out as gently as he could and collapsed onto the grass, taking Cory with him. Cory curled around him without a word, an arm around his middle and a leg thrown across his thighs. They lay like that for a long time, not talking, just holding each other. Paul closed his eyes and combed his fingers through Cory's damp curls. He felt he could happily stay there forever, sprawled on the grass in the dappled sunlight under the oaks with Cory warm and naked in his arms. He drew a deep breath of humid, salt-and-sex scented air, enjoying the feel of the summer heat pressing against his skin.

After a while, Paul roused himself from his doze with an effort and glanced at his watch. His eyes widened when he saw they'd been lying there nearly ten minutes. *It's a wonder Cory hasn't hauled both our asses up yet,* he thought with a chuckle. He knew Cory had the lunchtime kayak tour, and Mrs. Harrison would be arriving before long.

"Hey, Cory," Paul said, stroking Cory's back, "I think we'd better get up now."

No answer. Cory didn't move a muscle. Paul picked up Cory's hand. It lay limp and heavy in his own, fingers curled, and Paul realized that Cory had fallen asleep. He smiled, brought Cory's hand to his mouth and kissed his fingers one by one. Much as he hated to wake Cory, he knew he had to. Cory would never forgive him if he didn't.

"Cory?" Paul gave Cory's shoulder a gentle shake. "Wake up."

Cory stirred, opened his eyes, and lifted his head to blink sleepily at Paul. "Hm? What?"

Paul caressed Cory's cheek. "We fell asleep. I didn't want to wake you, but Mrs. Harrison will be here soon. We need to get up and get dressed."

"Oh, shit." Cory pushed to his feet, snatching up his shorts on the way. "How long was I asleep?"

"Only a few minutes." Paul stood slowly and started pulling on his shorts and T-shirt. "Hey, don't worry. We've still got a little while before Mrs. Harrison gets here."

Cory shot him a reproachful look as he zipped up his cutoffs. "Yeah, but I still have to finish hanging out the wash, and the carpet in the living room needs vacuuming, and I'm already late getting Mama turned, and—"

Paul stopped Cory with a hand against his lips. "It's okay. I'll help you finish up."

He moved his hand, and Cory gave him a sheepish grin. "You don't have to. Sorry. It's just, there's so much to do, you know, and I felt bad about falling asleep like that. I didn't mean to."

It made Paul's chest hurt to hear that. He pulled Cory into his arms, stroking the soft golden skin of his back with both palms. "Don't feel bad. You need every little bit of rest you can get. You're wearing yourself out." He lifted Cory's chin and kissed him before he could say anything. "And I want to help you, you know that. Besides, it's kind of my fault that you fell asleep right then, wasn't it?"

Cory laughed. "Okay, you talked me into it. We'll finish hanging out the laundry first, c'mon."

"Don't you have a dryer?"

"Yeah. But it broke down, and it's not something I can fix myself." Cory sighed as he secured a pillowcase to the line with clothespins. "Matter of fact, I'm not sure it *can* be fixed. And I sure as hell can't afford a new one. No big deal, though. My grandma dried clothes on the line, I guess I can too."

Paul hefted a blanket over the line without a word. He knew that what he had to say wouldn't be welcomed. They finished the job in silence. Paul's unspoken offer hung in the air between them. The tension in Paul's shoulders eased a little when Cory kissed him and looped an arm around his waist as they headed inside.

The second they stepped through the door, Paul knew something wasn't right. It took him a few seconds to figure out what it was. A faint rattling sound floated from the direction of the bedrooms. He and Cory looked at each other.

"What's that noise?" Paul asked.

Cory shook his head. "Don't know."

They headed toward the hall hand in hand. The noise grew louder as they went. When they reached the door of Lorraine's bedroom, Cory let out a cry and stumbled to his mother's side.

Paul stood rooted in the doorway, staring. Lorraine's body was shaking so hard that the headboard rattled against the wall. Her lips had a bluish tinge. A stream of yellow-green liquid ran from her mouth, soaking the neck of her thin gown and puddling on the pillow. The room smelled strongly of vomit.

Cory rolled his mother onto her side. He turned wide, frantic eyes to Paul. "Call 911, she's having a seizure!"

Paul ran into the kitchen and grabbed the phone, then ran back, dialing as he went. He described what had happened and gave the address in as calm a tone as he could manage. The seizure stopped before he was finished. After he hung up, he set the phone on the bedside table and laid a hand on Cory's shoulder. Cory jerked like he'd been burned. Paul dropped his hand again. His throat felt tight.

"Cory?"

Cory didn't even look at him. "Would you get me some towels or something? To clean her up with?"

Cory's voice was soft and broken. Paul wanted to say something, something that would take away the pain in

Cory's voice and make it right again. But there was nothing to say. He turned and went to find towels.

⊞ ⊞ ⊞

They worked in silence, Paul following Cory's terse instructions. By the time the ambulance arrived five minutes later, they'd gotten the worst of the mess cleaned up. Paul met the paramedics at the door and led them to the bedroom. Lorraine's body continued to twitch as the two young women examined her and moved her onto the stretcher. Her breathing sounded wet and labored behind the oxygen mask they strapped to her face.

"We're taking her to Hartsville Memorial," one of the paramedics said as they loaded the stretcher into the back of the ambulance. "You know how to get there?"

Cory drew a shaking breath. "Can...can I ride with her?"

The women looked at each other. "Well, you can if you don't have a ride. But it's pretty cramped back there, and I'll need to be able to maneuver, so it'd be better for you to just follow us, if you can."

Cory glanced at Paul, then stared at the ground. "Paul, can you..."

"Of course." Paul brushed his fingers over the back of Cory's hand. Cory pulled away, eyes still fixed on the grass under his feet. Paul clamped firmly down on his hurt and made himself meet the paramedic's gaze. "I'll drive him. I know where the hospital is."

The young woman gave a curt nod. "Okay. Don't worry if you lose us, you won't have any trouble since you know how to get there. And we'll tell the ER that Ms. Saunders' son is on the way."

"All right. Thank you."

Paul started toward the truck on rubbery legs. Cory followed him and climbed into the passenger seat. The ambulance pulled out of the driveway, sirens wailing, and Paul swung in behind it. He concentrated on the road and tried to ignore the gulf that yawned between himself and the young man huddled in the seat beside him. Cory's feeling were plain as day, in spite of his silence. Paul longed to erase that lost look from Cory's face, but he didn't know how. Nothing he could think of to say could possibly be adequate. So he said nothing, and they followed the ambulance in painful silence.

Paul let Cory out at the ER entrance and went to park the truck. After circling the packed parking lot three times, he finally spotted a Cadillac leaving. He pulled into the space and jogged toward the emergency-room doors, cursing under his breath. He found Cory leaning against the nurses' station desk, a phone receiver pressed to his ear. Cory glanced up as he approached, gaze darting quickly away again. Paul stood awkwardly beside him.

"Yeah, they're working on her now," Cory said softly into the phone. "They chased me out. Said they'd let me come back in as soon as they could, but she's not breathing too good right now... I don't know, they're giving her something to stop the seizures first... Yeah, I think so... They said they need to get a brain scan, but they have to get her stabilized first, and..." Cory sniffed deeply, his free hand absently rubbing his temple. "Sorry, I just... What? Oh, yeah, I'm okay, don't worry... Uh-huh... Sure, I'll call you as soon as I know anything else... Okay... Bye, Mrs. Harrison. Thanks."

Cory hung up and stood staring at the wall, chewing his thumbnail. Paul wanted badly to pull Cory into his arms, hold him and stroke his hair and tell him everything was going to be all right. But he didn't think Cory would welcome his embrace. And of course, nothing was all right. He couldn't just stand there and watch Cory quietly tearing himself apart, though. He took a deep breath.

"Cory, I'm sorry," he said, the words coming out in a rush. "I know what you're thinking, but you know it wouldn't have made any difference if we—"

"You don't know that," Cory interrupted. "Maybe it would've. Maybe if I'd gone inside when I was supposed to, I would've been there when she started having seizures."

"And then what? Could you have stopped her from having them?" Paul laid a tentative hand on Cory's arm. "Come on, Cory, don't do this."

Cory yanked his arm away and started pacing. "What else am I supposed to think, Paul? If I'd been in there earlier, I could've at least kept her from getting vomit in her lungs. She could die from this! All because I couldn't keep my fucking pants on. How the fuck am I supposed to live with that?"

Paul swallowed against the sudden ache in his throat. "If you want to blame someone, blame me, not yourself. I'm the one who came barging in and talked you into...doing what we did. I'm so sorry, Cory."

Cory stopped pacing and pinned Paul with a look full of anguish. "How could I blame you? I wanted it just as bad as you did. And I was the one who was supposed to be...to be r-responsible... Shit..."

Cory took a few gulping breaths, eyes wide and fixed on the ceiling, hugging himself so hard his arms trembled. He shook his head and stepped back when Paul reached for him. Paul stood and watched helplessly as Cory fought to get his emotions under control.

Paul shoved his hands in his shorts pockets, to keep himself from touching Cory since he clearly didn't want it. "Is there anything I can do to help? You want me to call work for you?"

"No, I'll do it." Cory swiped a hand across his eyes. He wouldn't look at Paul. "You can go now, if you want. Mrs. Harrison's coming on over."

"Oh. Okay, I guess I'll...go, then. If that's what you want." Paul hated the quaver in his voice, but he couldn't stop it.

Cory looked right at him, eyes wet and hurting. "Thanks for driving me over here, Paul, but I think I'd like to you leave now. Sorry."

Paul shook his head, letting his hair fall over his eyes to hide what he was feeling. "No, it's okay. Just...call me, huh? If you need me?"

Cory didn't answer. Paul watched for a minute as Cory picked up the phone and started dialing. When it became clear that he was indeed dismissed, Paul turned and headed out the door. He felt numb all over. Miraculously, his legs carried him all the way to his truck without collapsing under him.

He managed to get home, though he didn't remember the trip. All he could think of was the look on Cory's face when they walked in and found his mother in the throes of that seizure. Fear, and pain, and a soul-deep guilt. That one moment had changed everything. It scared Paul to know that the chasm it had created between them might be too wide to bridge.

Paul stumbled inside and flung himself onto the bed, curling into a ball, trying to hold himself together. "Shit, Cory," he whispered. "Shit."

He lay there, shaking and cursing himself, until exhaustion finally caught up with him and he slept. His dreams were filled with the rattling of the headboard and the smell of vomit, and green eyes that still didn't blame him, no matter how much he wanted them to.

CHAPTER NINE

Cory woke to the sound of soft sobs. He opened his eyes, stretched, and uncurled himself from the chair he'd been sleeping in for the last four days. On the other side of the ICU waiting room, a middle-aged couple clung together, crying. One of the hospital chaplains sat beside them, holding their hands and murmuring something Cory couldn't hear.

Cory leaned toward the sofa beside his chair, where Alicia sat flipping through a magazine. "Hey, 'Licia."

She looked up at him. "It's still an hour 'til visiting time, Cory, go on back to sleep."

Cory sighed. Alicia had been a downright nag the last few days about how little sleep he was getting. He wondered what she'd say if she knew he'd slept more since Mama had been in the hospital than he had for weeks before that.

"Naw, I'm good." Cory gestured toward the sobbing couple. "She didn't make it, did she?"

Alicia shook her head. "No. She died in surgery."

"Oh." Cory's heart ached for the man and woman who'd just lost their only child. They'd come in the night before, faces blank with shock, their seventeen-year-old daughter near death after being hit by a boat while water skiing. "God, that's awful."

"Yeah." Alicia reached out and took Cory's hand. "Whenever the rest of their family gets here, I'll see about sending some food to their place from Uncle Charlie's."

Cory nodded, throat too tight to speak. He'd only just met the couple, but like everyone else in this little room, they'd quickly become family. The fear and worry and heartache they had in common brought them together, giving them all a strength they didn't have on their own. Cory was grateful for that. The odd camaraderie of the ICU waiting room had helped sustain him through the past four days. Alicia and Mrs. Harrison had taken it upon themselves to wait with him in shifts every day, and he loved them for it. But he never would've survived the long nights without these people who knew what it was to live in limbo, waiting for those fifteen minutes, five times a day, when they were allowed to see the people they loved.

There was no ICU visiting between ten p.m. and six a.m., and the nights lasted forever.

"Saw Paul yesterday."

Alicia's voice was casual, but Cory knew better. He pulled his hand out of hers and wrapped both arms around his knees. "That's nice."

"He asked about you. And your mom."

Cory stared steadfastly at the carpet. "Oh, yeah?"

"Mm-hm." Pages crinkled as Alicia tossed the magazine aside. "What the hell happened, Cory? Why isn't he ever here with you?"

"How should I know? Ask him."

Cory knew he sounded childish and petulant, but he couldn't help it. Any mention of Paul seemed to put him on the defensive. He desperately missed Paul's kiss, Paul's arms around him, those eyes that looked at him with such tenderness. But thoughts of Paul brought with them a crippling guilt, and a shame that made his cheeks burn. His mother had depended on him to take care of her, and he'd let her down. He hadn't told anyone what had happened that day. The knowledge lay like a stone in his guts.

Alicia sighed. "I did ask him. He said he thought it was better if he didn't come."

"Oh."

Cory felt Alicia's eyes on him. He remained stubbornly silent. She made an impatient noise, grabbed his arm and shook him none-too-gently. "Fucking look at me, Cory."

Cory turned just enough to give his friend a sidelong look through the hair that fell over his face. She frowned at him, brown eyes snapping.

"You don't want to tell me what's going on between you and Paul? Fine, whatever." Alicia's voice was low and angry. "But let me tell *you* something, boy. You beating yourself up over whatever it is you think you've done isn't helping anyone, least of all your mother. You think she'd want to see you like this? Hell no, she'd want you to be happy. That's all she ever wanted."

Cory laughed, the sound sharp and bitter. "You don't know what I did, 'Licia."

"Did you try to kill her?"

"No!" He sat up and stared, shocked to the core.

Alicia stared right back, lips twisting into a humorless smile. "Then what the fuck do you have to feel guilty about, huh?"

Cory sat perfectly still, trying to breathe past the sudden hollowness in his chest. His insides seethed with fear and anger and sorrow and the guilt he couldn't help feeling. Somewhere in a calm corner of his mind, he knew Alicia was right. He just couldn't make himself believe it yet.

He held his hand out. Alicia took it, like he knew she would. Neither of them said anything more, but Cory knew she understood.

☒   ☒   ☒

Alicia left after the two o'clock visiting period for the dinner shift at Uncle Charlie's. Mrs. Harrison arrived half an hour later, the big canvas bag with her knitting in it tucked under her arm. She gave Cory a smile and a pat on the cheek before settling onto the sofa to work on the sweater she was knitting for her husband. Cory curled up in the chair, dozing on and off as the afternoon sun stretched lengthening shadows across the room.

He was dreaming of Paul's hands on his skin when Mrs. Harrison shook him gently awake. "Cory? It's visiting time, honey."

He sat up, yawning. "Okay, thanks." An image from his dream flashed through his mind—soft lips trailing down his neck, blue eyes hot and needy, *God so good...* His head whirled with desire and guilt and something else, something he wasn't sure he wanted to examine too closely. He bit his lip, staring down at his lap and trying like hell to hide the turmoil inside him.

Mrs. Harrison turned her sharp brown gaze on him. "You all right? You want me to come with you?"

He shook his head. "No, it's okay. I'm fine." He made himself meet her eyes, and gave her a slightly shaky smile. "Thanks for being here. It means a lot to me."

"Glad I can help out, baby." She patted his hand with her cool, dry fingers. "Now you run on. Tell Lorraine I asked after her."

"'Kay." Cory stood, knees wobbling a little. "Be back in a little bit."

Cory could've sworn the hallway to the ICU got longer every day. He joined the throng of people talking in hushed tones outside the big double doors, waiting for the nurses to let them in. Some had been caught in this routine for days or weeks, others for only hours, but all had the same stunned, hollow-eyed expression. Cory hadn't looked in a mirror in days, not even when Alicia dragged him back to her apartment and made him shower. He didn't want to see that dead look in his own eyes.

When the day-shift charge nurse opened the doors, Cory shuffled in along with everyone else. He waited his turn at the sink beside the door, washed his hands, and headed straight for Mama's bedside.

"Hi, Mama." He bent and kissed her cheek before settling into the chair. "Mrs. Harrison's here. She says tell you she's thinking of you."

He lapsed into silence, absently stroking the back of his mother's hand and thinking, remembering all the good times and bad times they'd been through together. Riding bikes to the ice-cream place down the road, finger-painting at the kitchen table, making up crazy games to pass the time while they worked in the house or the yard. Birthdays and Christmases and summer afternoons at the beach. Mama trying so hard not to cry at Granny's funeral, trying to be strong for him. That night in tenth grade when he'd waited up for her to get home from the late shift at the hospital and told her he was gay. Shock and pain and disappointment had fleeted through her eyes so fast he wasn't even sure he'd seen it, then she'd smiled and hugged him and told him that he was who he was and she loved him no matter what.

He was so lost in his thoughts, fifteen minutes passed before he knew it. As he stood to leave, Mama's nurse leaned into the doorway. "Cory? Dr. Vasquez is here. He'd like to talk to you."

"Oh. Sure, okay." Cory kissed his mother's fingers. "Bye, Mama. I'll see you at ten. Love you."

Dr. Vasquez stood waiting at the nurses' station. He'd been Mama's neurosurgeon since the start, knew her case better than almost anyone, but Cory had never felt easy in his presence. Something about the man put him on edge. He wished he could talk to Mama's regular internist, Dr. Bishop. Her sweet, friendly manner always calmed Cory, let him think. Dr. Vasquez just made him feel tense.

"Hello, Cory," Dr. Vasquez said, smiling.

Cory shook the hand he was offered. "Hi, Dr. Vasquez. You wanted to see me?"

"Yes, I did. There's something I'd like to discuss with you." The doctor nodded toward the private conference room next to the nurses' station. "Let's go sit down, hm?"

Cory followed Dr. Vasquez into the conference room and perched on the edge of a chair, picking at the hole in the knee of his jeans. The surgeon's solemn expression made him nervous. "What's up?"

Dr. Vasquez sat down in the other chair and leaned forward, long hands clasped together in his lap. "Cory, I'm going to be perfectly honest with you. Your mother's prognosis is grim. The CT scan shows multiple new lesions throughout her brain. Probably more tumors, though of course it's impossible to know for sure without a biopsy. She also has aspiration pneumonia in both lungs, and her kidneys are beginning to fail."

Cory stared at a scuff mark on the white tile floor. "So what do we do?"

"I think it's time to consider taking her off of the ventilator, making her as comfortable as we can, and letting her go."

Cory's head snapped up, heart pounding. "You mean just let her die?"

"I don't mean to be harsh, Cory, but your mother is not going to live much longer, no matter what we do. Her body is shutting down. We can keep her alive with the vent, drugs, and tube feedings for a while, but it wouldn't be more than a few weeks at most, much less than that if we can't get the pneumonia under control. And she would have to remain right here in the ICU the entire time."

Cory twisted his fingers together, fighting the urge to put his fist through the wall. It was just so fucking unfair. "I... I need to..." He drew a deep breath. "Do I have to decide right now?"

"No, of course not." The doctor stood, dark brown eyes regarding him thoughtfully. "This is a difficult decision, and shouldn't be made lightly. Take whatever time you need. Think it over, and let me know what you want to do, okay?"

Cory nodded, not trusting himself to speak. After Dr. Vasquez left, he sat there for a long time, staring at the painting of sand dunes hanging on the wall and wondering where the hell he was supposed to find the strength to watch his mother die.

❖ ❖ ❖

Mrs. Harrison knew something was wrong. Cory could tell by the way she looked at him. Of course, he'd been away for nearly forty-five minutes instead of fifteen, so he figured he'd given her ample reason to worry. He made up a vague excuse about running into an old friend, then curled up in his usual chair and pretended to sleep. Eventually she packed up her knitting, dropped a gentle kiss on his brow, and left.

He wasn't sure why he didn't tell her what Dr. Vasquez said. She would've listened without judgment, and guided him without letting her own views color his decision. He sure as hell could've used the help. But he hadn't said a word. Maybe talking about it made it too real. Or maybe he simply had to carry this particular burden alone.

The night nurse took pity on him when he begged to be allowed to stay after the ten p.m. visitation was over. He spent the night beside his mother's bed, in blatant disregard of hospital rules, holding Mama's limp hand in his and thinking. He told himself that he was trying to decide what was best for Mama. But the reality of it was, he was trying to work up the courage to do what he knew in his heart was right.

Mama's chest rose and fell with the artificial rhythm of the ventilator, her heartbeat showed reassuringly steady on the monitor, but the spark was gone, and had been for a long time. All the little things and big things that made her who she was had leeched away, leaving only a shell behind. She'd never wanted that, and Cory knew it.

It was time to let her go.

▨   ▨   ▨

The night was long and sleepless. By the time the sky outside began to lighten, Cory felt wrung out and exhausted, but resolute. Hard as it was, he believed his decision was the right one.

To Cory's surprise, Mrs. Harrison showed up for the six a.m. visiting period. He greeted her with a hug and a tired smile. "You didn't have to come so early, you know. But I'm glad you did."

She squeezed his hand. "You were doing some hard thinking yesterday, Cory. Thought you might've made up your mind at last, and you might want a friend to be with you when the time comes."

He blinked at her. "How'd you know?"

Her smile was sad. "Honey, you're not the first to have to decide that it's time to let go. I've seen it more times than I care to remember. I know the signs."

Cory's throat constricted. He wandered over to lean against the windowsill, watching the early morning light sparkle in the dewy grass. "She wouldn't have wanted to live this way."

"I know, baby."

"So it's right, isn't it?" Cory turned to look into Mrs. Harrison's calm brown eyes. "I'm doing the right thing?"

"That's up to you and the good Lord. But for what it's worth, I believe you're doing right by your mama." Mrs. Harrison came to him and laid her hands on his shoulders. "I know it's hard, Cory. Nothing harder in this world. But it's what your mama would want."

Cory nodded. He wished his hands would stop shaking. "Will you stay with me? Dr. Vasquez'll be in before long, and I want...I want to..."

He couldn't finish, but he didn't need to. Mrs. Harrison slipped a hand through his elbow and led him to the chair, gently pushing him down into it before he could object. "I'll stay, honey."

While she went out to the nurses' station to ask for another chair, Cory scooted up close to the bed and took his mother's hand. "It's almost over, Mama," he whispered, laying her palm against his cheek. "I love you."

He leaned against the bed rail and wished, not for the first time, that he had the courage to ask Paul to come back.

CHAPTER TEN

The green, Paul thought, still wasn't quite right. He frowned. Maybe a lighter shade this time. He picked up a miniscule dollop of pale gold with the tip of his brush and dabbed tiny streaks around the pupils of the painted irises. He took a step back and nodded. Perfect. The gold added just the right touch.

He cleaned his brushes and put away the oils, then sat down on the studio sofa to examine his latest painting. Cory smiled back at him from the canvas, green eyes warm and bright and achingly real. Something inside Paul twisted. It was one of the finest pieces he'd ever painted, and he could barely look at it. This one hurt worse than any of the others.

"It's the green," Paul whispered. "I finally got it right."

He'd been trying for days. Ever since that afternoon at the hospital, he'd spent most of his time in his studio, painting portrait after portrait. Cory lying naked on the sofa, Cory gazing out the window, Cory laughing in the long yellow grass behind his house. All excellent work, none of it quite right. This time, he'd done it. He'd captured the gilded green of Cory's eyes to perfection.

He wished like hell he hadn't. It brought back that day with an intensity that tore at his guts.

He leaned back and covered his face with both hands. No matter how hard he tried, he hadn't been able to erase the memories. He couldn't forget the pure happiness of dozing in Cory's arms any more than he could forget that stricken look on Cory's face. He'd have given anything to change that one awful moment, and take away the guilt in Cory's eyes.

He'd been on the verge of going to the hospital any number of times. He longed to talk to Cory, to know if he was all right. He'd be halfway to his truck, determined to do it this time. Then he'd hear Cory telling him to leave, he'd see Cory turning away from him, and he'd stop himself. Seeing Cory would be purely selfish on his part, if Cory didn't want him there. And it seemed pretty clear that he didn't. He surely would've called if he did.

Paul took an odd satisfaction in the realization that Cory must blame him after all. He much preferred that to having Cory blame himself.

"Stop it," Paul hissed at the ceiling. "Just fucking stop."

If only it were that easy to halt the endless circular arguments going on in his head. He pushed himself up off the couch and left the studio without another glance at the painting. The grass needed mowing, and there were three days' worth of dirty dishes in the sink. Maybe a little hard work would settle his mind and soothe the ache in his chest. It was sure as hell worth a try.

Six hours later, damp and relaxed after his shower, Paul sank down into the lawn chair out back with a grateful sigh. The grass was cut, the entire house sparkled, and he'd even washed and waxed the old truck. He was blissfully tired. He took a long swallow of ice water and gazed thoughtfully out over the meadow. The pines across the river formed a shadowy silhouette against the red-orange sky.

Cory would love this. He could practically see Cory now, standing on the edge of the meadow with his hands in the pockets of those ragged cutoffs he always wore, eyes shining as he exclaimed over the fiery beauty of the sunset. The longing to hold Cory right then was overwhelming. Paul closed his eyes and gave himself up to the memory of Cory's arms around him, Cory's lips warm and soft against his, Cory's smooth tanned skin bare and flushed with desire.

The ringing of the phone brought him abruptly out of his thoughts. He jumped up and ran inside to answer it, mentally cursing whoever had interrupted his fantasy.

He snatched the receiver out of the cradle with far more force than was necessary. "Hello?"

"Paul?"

Everything went still. Paul had to force himself to speak. "Cory. Are you all right?"

"She's gone, Paul. I let them take her off the vent, and, and..." Cory let out a strange, harsh sound. "Paul, please come. Please."

Cory sounded lost and broken. Paul wanted to jump right through the phone line, hold him and kiss him and take the hurt out of his voice. He gripped the phone hard. "I can be there in a few minutes. Where are you?"

"ICU. II'm sorry."Paul didn't know what Cory was sorry for. He had a feeling Cory wasn't sure himself. "There's nothing to be sorry for, Cory. Hang on, okay? I'm coming."

Cory's whispered thank you was cut short by the phone being hung up. Paul stood frozen for a moment, listening to the silence on the other end. He dropped the receiver back into the cradle, grabbed his wallet and keys and ran for the truck.

▨   ▨   ▨

It was in between visiting times when Paul arrived at Hartsville Memorial's intensive care unit, and the ward clerk who answered when he rang the buzzer didn't want to let him in. Luckily, the charge nurse had been told to expect him, so he didn't have to resort to busting the doors down.

Mrs. Harrison stood at the desk, talking in low tones to one of the nurses. He hurried over to her, and she hugged him. "Paul, I'm so glad you came."

"I'm glad he finally called me," Paul answered, kissing her cheek. "What happened?"

"Cory agreed to take Lorraine off life support and let her go. It was the best thing to do. She always said not to try and keep her when her time came. But it was a hard decision for him to make. That boy loves his mama." She sighed. Paul squeezed her hand and she gave him a grateful smile. "It was quick, thank the Lord. They took her off the vent 'bout six hours ago. She passed peacefully just a few minutes before Cory called you. He was right there with her, holding her hand."

"I'm glad he was with her. I hope it helped."

"It did. Even if he can't see it yet. Once some time has passed and he can look at things a little more clearly, he'll be happy he could be with her when she passed on."

Paul stared at the floor, fighting a hurt that was all too familiar. Jay had died alone, without Paul there to comfort him and ease his passing. The pain of it never left Paul entirely, and now it felt like a knife in the gut. His heart ached for Cory, but he was profoundly grateful that Cory had been with his mother when she died.

Mrs. Harrison laid a cool hand on his arm. "You okay, Paul?"

He nodded and forced a smile. "Yeah, fine. Where's Cory? Can I see him now?"

"Room ten, right over there." She pointed to a glass door on the other side of the ICU. The curtain was drawn, preventing anyone from seeing in. "Paul?"

Paul tore his gaze from the door and met Mrs. Harrison's eyes. "Yes?"

"You take good care of him, you hear? He needs you."

"I will. I promise."

She smiled at him. "Thank you. Now I have to go. The funeral home'll be coming soon to take Lorraine, and my James is waiting for me to pick him up from his brother's house. You tell Cory to call me tomorrow."

"Okay. Bye, Mrs. Harrison. Thank you."

She patted his cheek, hoisted her purse over her shoulder, and left, calling goodbyes to the nurses. Paul took a deep breath and headed toward room ten.

The little cubicle was dim, lit mostly by the night-light built into the bottom of the bed frame. The sunset had faded to a dull red that glinted off Cory's disheveled curls. Cory sat on the side of his mother's bed, stroking her hair and whispering something Paul couldn't quite hear.

Paul approached slowly, not sure what to say. He knew from experience that comforting words were worse than useless. Only time could dull the pain Cory was feeling. Paul sat on the edge of the chair, facing Cory, and laid a hand on his knee.

"Cory, I'm here," he said, keeping his voice soft.

Cory spoke without looking up, his voice slow and even. "It's not fair, Paul. It's just not fucking fair."

"No, it isn't." Paul swallowed hard, wishing he had the right words. "I'm so sorry."

Cory lifted his head and stared at Paul with haunted eyes. "Can I stay with you tonight?"

"Of course you can. Stay as long as you need to."

Cory didn't say another word. He turned his gaze back to his mother's face. One hand kept combing through her hair. His other hand crept into Paul's, and Paul held on tight.

◈　　◈　　◈

Two workers from Thomlinson's Funeral Home in Willow Bend showed up ten minutes later. Cory kissed his mother's brow and whispered something against her cheek, then calmly stood aside while the man and woman gently lifted her onto a special gurney and wheeled her out of the room. Cory stared after them, silent and strangely blank-faced, until they were out of sight. He kept his fingers firmly locked through Paul's.

Paul reached out to brush a lock of tangled hair away from Cory's face. "Cory? Why don't we go now, huh?"

Cory nodded. He said nothing, but allowed Paul to lead him out of the ICU.

They walked out to the parking lot in silence, still holding hands, and climbed into Paul's truck. Paul fastened Cory's seatbelt for him when he made no move to do it himself. Throughout the short trip to Paul's house, Cory sat staring out the window at the deepening night, not saying a word. Paul kept darting worried glances at him. Cory's listless quiet made him uneasy.

Paul parked the truck on the gravel drive just outside the front door rather than in the barn, wanting to get Cory inside and settled as quickly as possible. He went around to Cory's side, unlatched his seatbelt, and took his hand. "We're here, Cory. Come on, let's get you inside."

Cory slid obediently out of the truck and followed Paul into the house. Paul led him to the bedroom, flipping on lights as he went. Cory sat on the bed while Paul dug a clean pair of soft knit shorts and a T-shirt out of his dresser drawers.

"Here," he said, laying the clothes beside Cory. "Figured you might want to change."

Cory stared at the clothes for a moment, then lifted his empty eyes to Paul's face. "Can I shower first?"

"Yeah, sure." Paul hurried toward the bathroom, berating himself for not having offered Cory a shower already. He pulled a big, fluffy towel out of the linen closet and hung it over the rack next to the tub, then went back into the bedroom. "You need me to help you?"

Cory shook his head. He stood, picked up the clean clothes, and shuffled into the bathroom, leaving the door halfway open. A moment later, Paul heard the shower start up.

He flopped into the big armchair with a deep sigh. Cory's peculiar behavior had him more than a little worried. He'd expected tears at least, maybe even grief-stricken rage. God knows that's how he himself had reacted when he'd woken up after five days in intensive care to learn that Jay was dead and buried. He'd torn his IVs out and thrown things and screamed in spite of his bruised, weak lungs, cursing the world and everyone in it for taking Jay away from him without even letting him say goodbye. He hadn't stopped until they'd given him the shot that sent him into welcome unconsciousness.

Terrible as it would be to witness, Paul would've preferred that sort of reaction. Cory's dry-eyed silence frightened him.

It had been more than fifteen minutes and Paul was starting to wonder if he should go in and check, when he heard an odd strangled noise, followed by a dull thud. His heart leapt into his throat.

"Cory?" he called, crossing to the bathroom in a few strides. "Cory, are you... Oh."

The sight that met Paul's eyes was heartbreaking. Cory sat on the floor of the tub, knees drawn up to his chest, with one hand pressed flat against the tile wall and the other clenched in his hair. Water pounded down on his bowed head and shoulders. His delicate features were twisted with agony.

Paul turned the water off, then climbed into the tub, clothes and all, and folded Cory into his arms. Cory let out a soft little choking sound. He threw his arms around Paul's neck, clutching with desperate strength. Paul hauled Cory into his lap and held him as tight as he could. Cory buried his face in the curve of Paul's neck, his body shaking with deep, ragged sobs.

It hurt horribly to see Cory suffering such grief. But these were the kind of tears powerful enough to purge some of the pain, and Paul felt the tightness inside him ease. Cory would be okay. He was letting himself grieve, and he would be okay.

Eventually, the sobs quieted and Cory's tense body began to relax. Paul lifted Cory's chin, searching his red and swollen eyes. "You okay?"

A ghost of a smile touched Cory's lips. "Better. Sorry."

"No. No apologizing to me." Paul ran his fingers down Cory's cheek. "Cry when you need to. Or yell, or talk, or whatever you need to do. I'll be here."

"I know." Cory slid a hand behind Paul's head and pulled him closer. "Thank you."

Paul wanted to cry when Cory's lips pressed to his. He'd missed Cory's kiss so much. He didn't try to take it any further. Cory needed comfort and care from him, not sex.

Cory broke the kiss and leaned his forehead against Paul's. Paul laid a hand on his cheek. "I bet you're worn out. Why don't you go on to bed?"

"Yeah. That sounds good." Cory pulled back, green eyes pleading. "Can I sleep with you? I don't think I can go to sleep by myself."

"Sure." Paul nudged Cory off his lap, stood, and helped Cory to his feet. "Come on, let's get dried off."

Most of the water had already evaporated off Cory's skin by that time, but he let Paul rub his dripping curls with the towel until they were nearly dry. Paul was surprised when Cory left the clothes and got into bed naked. He smiled, stripped off his own damp clothes, and crawled under the covers. Cory wrapped himself around Paul, resting his head on Paul's chest.

"'Night," Cory murmured drowsily.

"Goodnight." Paul kissed the top of Cory's head. "Sleep well."

Cory mumbled something and pressed closer, his body already relaxing into sleep. Paul traced his fingers up and down Cory's spine, the motion soothing for him as much as for Cory. It felt good to hold Cory while he slept, even if the reason why he could was a terrible one. The thought gave him a twinge of guilt, wondering if it were wrong to feel so good when Cory had just been through one of the worst experiences of his life.

No. No more guilt. He figured he and Cory had earned the right to enjoy every good thing that came their way. He closed his eyes and leaned his cheek against Cory's soft curls.

This time, he didn't try to deny what he felt. He knew it was true, and he knew it was right.

CHAPTER ELEVEN

Cory woke with a pounding headache. He opened his eyes carefully since he expected the morning light to make his head hurt worse. The room was blessedly dark. His eyes felt swollen, his throat raw. For a second he thought he must have caught the summer cold that had been working its way through the town lately. Then everything came back in a rush that made his chest hurt.

He closed his eyes again and snuggled closer to Paul. They'd shifted positions sometime in the night, and Paul's nude body was molded to Cory's back, arms firmly around his waist. It felt good to be held like that. It felt even better to know that he could count on Paul to be there when he needed him.

His memories of the previous day were jumbled and incoherent, like a film cut up and spliced back together with the scenes out of order. Mrs. Harrison's face, calm and sad and tear-streaked. The tortured rasp of Mama's breathing becoming slow and shallow, and finally ceasing altogether. Mama's soft, fine hair between his fingers. A final whispered goodbye and "I love you" when they came to take her away. Single vivid moments that felt at once intense and oddly distant.

Then there was Paul. The one thing that seemed real and solid in that whole nightmarish day. The second he'd picked up the phone to call Paul's house, he'd known it was the right thing to do. He hadn't thought about it, hadn't let himself question it. He'd just done it. And Paul had come without hesitation, giving him an anchor in a suddenly shifting world.

A world that now lay wide open before him. A world of time and space and no responsibilities, except to himself.

The realization hit Cory like a slap in the face. He squirmed out of Paul's sleeping embrace, ran silently into the bathroom, and threw up.

It didn't take long for his stomach to empty completely. He hadn't eaten anything at all the previous day, and not much for a while before that. When his shaking subsided, he stood carefully, flushed the toilet, and splashed cold water on his face. Using his finger as a toothbrush, he borrowed some of Paul's toothpaste and scrubbed the acrid taste out of his mouth as well as he could.

He didn't look at his reflection for long. What he saw— hollow cheeks, stubbled chin, haunted and black-shadowed eyes—made him shudder. He tiptoed back into the bedroom, pulled on the clothes Paul had left out for him the night before, and went outside.

The sky to the east had just begun to pale when he stepped out onto the front porch. Birds trilled in the trees, a truck rumbled down the road beyond Paul's driveway. Cory wandered down the path to the barn, letting the early morning stillness soak into him. In the dimness of the old barn, he hesitated for only a moment before climbing the ladder to Paul's loft studio.

Cory's jaw dropped when he reached the top. "Oh. Oh, wow."

He stepped off the ladder, eyes wide and heart pounding. His own face stared back at him from at least ten canvases. Smiling, or pensive, or flushed with sex, his body clothed in some, naked in others. It was the first time Cory had seen Paul's work. It was beyond impressive.

Cory wandered around, examining each painting. They were stunning. He could practically feel the hot, humid breeze ruffling the painted trees and grasses. He almost expected his image to move when he wasn't looking. Every detail was perfectly rendered.

There was something about the paintings, though. A magical sort of shine, as if the eye that envisioned them had been less than objective. When he realized what it meant, he sat down hard in the middle of the floor, feeling like he'd been punched.

The paintings seemed like idealized versions of him because that's exactly what they were.

Paul was in love with him.

🔲　🔲　🔲

Cory was still sitting there, lost in thought, when Paul found him a couple of hours later. He didn't look up when Paul stepped into the loft, afraid of what he might see in those white-blue eyes. Paul sat on the floor beside him and slipped an arm around his shoulders. Cory leaned gratefully into the embrace.

"You okay?" Paul said, his cheek resting against Cory's hair.

"Yeah."

"You could've woken me, you know."

He did know. The truth of that thrilled him, and scared him. "You needed to sleep. And I needed some time alone, to think about things."

Paul's arm tightened around him. "Feels strange, doesn't it? Having a person be a huge part of your life one day, and gone the next."

Cory's breath stuck in his chest. He nodded, tried to answer, and couldn't. An aching sadness welled up inside him. Not as sharp as it had been the night before, but more profound. Deep as the sea, wide as the horizon. This was a feeling that wouldn't go away in a hurry. He turned in Paul's embrace, wound both arms around him, and let the tears come.

Most people Cory knew, with the possible exception of Mrs. Harrison, would have smothered him with well-meaning concern. They'd tell him that at least Mama's suffering had finally ended, that she was in a better place. Not Paul. Paul just held him, without comment or judgment, and let him cry. He was desperately grateful for that. He didn't think he could face having to smile and nod and tell all the little lies people wanted to hear.

When the tears finally slowed, Cory sat up and gave Paul a wan smile. "Thanks."

"Sometimes you just have to let yourself feel it." Paul touched Cory's cheek, very gently. "You ever need someone to talk to, or just someone to cry on, I'm right here."

"I miss her, you know? I keep thinking about how she used to be, and I wish I could have her back." Cory stared at the floor. He scraped at a splatter of paint with his fingernail. "I don't care if it's better this way. I just want her back like she was before she got sick."

"Of course you do." Paul took Cory's hand in his. "Anybody would."

"Paul? Will you hate me if I tell you something awful?"

Paul didn't even hesitate. "Nothing could make me hate you, Cory. Tell me."

Cory took a deep breath, hoping Paul was right. "I...I'm sort of glad she died. And not because it's better for her or because it's what she would've wanted. I'm glad because now..."

He couldn't say it. But Paul seemed to understand. "You're glad," Paul said softly, "because now you're free to live your own life."

Somehow, it didn't surprise Cory that Paul knew.

"Why do I feel like that, Paul? Everything she ever did, she did for me, and now she's gone, she died because of *me* and I..." Cory drew a hitching breath. "I'm glad, Paul, I'm glad she died. God, what's *wrong* with me?"

"Cory. C'mere." Paul gathered Cory into his arms, settling him onto his lap. "Listen to me. Your mother was very sick for a long time. It had to hurt terribly to see her like that. Of course you'd be glad that's over. And you did everything humanly possible to take care of her, to the point where you weren't taking care of yourself. It was wearing you out. You couldn't have kept up that pace for much longer. It's only natural to be relieved that you won't have that workload anymore."

"Yeah, but..."

"Hey." Paul's eyes bored into his, so earnest it hurt. "Just because part of you is happy, doesn't mean that you're not sad about her dying, or that you didn't love her and won't miss her. You are, and you did, and you will. There's nothing wrong with being glad that a very difficult period of your life, and hers, is over."

A tiny smile tugged at the corners of Cory's mouth. "You make it sound so reasonable."

"It *is* reasonable."

Cory rested his head in the curve of Paul's neck. A strange, tight feeling burned in his chest. He thought he knew what it was, in spite of never having felt it before Paul came along. He wanted badly to tell Paul.

It took him a few minutes to realize, with a pleasant shock, that he could.

"Paul?"

"Hm?"

Cory shifted on Paul's lap, raised his head and looked straight into Paul's eyes. "I'm in love with you."

Paul blinked. "You... Oh. Oh, my God." He licked his lips, his wide, shocked eyes fixed on Cory's face. "Cory, you're going through a lot right now, it can all get you pretty confused, and—"

"No. I'm not confused. I'm really grateful to you for coming when I called, and for looking after me, and for everything else you've done for me ever since we met. But that's not why I'm saying this." Cory cupped Paul's face in his hands. "I'm not any more confused about my feelings than you are about yours."

The color drained from Paul's face. "What?"

"The paintings." Cory nodded at a portrait of himself standing on the beach at Otter Island. "Do you really love me, Paul?"

The heartbeat of silence that followed lasted eons. Cory let out the breath he'd been holding when Paul smiled at him.

"Yes," Paul said, his voice soft and husky. "I love you."

Hearing Paul say it made Cory feel warm and peaceful inside. He leaned forward and kissed Paul's lips. "Will you wait for me?"

"Wait for you?" Paul returned the kiss, one hand on Cory's cheek.

"I'm so tired. And I need a little time to think, before we...you know, start anything." Cory shut his eyes and leaned his forehead against Paul's. "Please say that's okay."

Paul didn't point out that it was far too late to worry about starting something, since they were already deep in it. Cory was glad. It made him feel foolish that the thought of making their relationship official scared him like it did, but he couldn't help it.

"Of course it's okay. There's no rush." Paul kissed him again and pulled back, happiness bright in his eyes. "C'mon, let's go back to the house. I'll fix us some breakfast."

They got up off the floor, climbed down the ladder, and headed back toward the house. Cory clung to Paul as hard as he could, grief and fear and relief and happiness making him shaky and lightheaded. The next few days were going to be hard. There were bills to pay, and lots of people he still had to call. He needed to talk to Alicia and the manager at Uncle Charlie's, he needed to call Willow Bend Outdoors. At some point, he needed to go back home, clean the place up. Go through Mama's things.

Oh, God.

He had to bury his mother.

Cory made a soft little heartbroken sound. Paul's arm tightened around him in silent reassurance, and Cory thought maybe he could face it after all.

CHAPTER TWELVE

"Paul!" Alicia called from the bedroom. "Get me the scrub brush, would you?"

"Sure thing," Paul yelled back. He leaned the mop against the wall, grabbed the plastic scrubber off the kitchen counter, and trotted into the bedroom. He handed the brush to Alicia with a smile. "Here."

"Thanks." She wiped the sweat off her brow with her forearm. Both hands dripped with soapy water from the bucket at her side. "Almost done here. How's the kitchen coming?"

"Fine. It was barely even dirty." Paul gestured at the spot of threadbare carpet that Alicia was cleaning. "This is the only room that really needed cleaning."

"Yeah. Between them, Cory and Mrs. Harrison keep a damn clean house."

Paul had to agree with that. When Alicia called that morning to check on Cory, Paul had asked her if she'd help him clean the house. She'd readily agreed. Both had expected more of a job. Other than Lorraine's bedroom, nothing much needed cleaning. An hour after they arrived, Paul had the whole place vacuumed and dusted, and Alicia had nearly gotten all of the greenish stain out of the bedroom carpet. Lorraine's mattress, however, they gave up as a lost cause. The stain might've come out

159

eventually, but it reeked of the vomit that had soaked right through into the interior.

"Hey, Paul?"

Paul blinked, realizing he'd been staring into space. "Yeah?"

Alicia's brown eyes were full of concern. "How is he? He says he's okay, but I know how stubborn he is."

"He'll be all right. He's completely worn out, and of course he's grieving for his mother. But he's coping." Paul sighed. "I think he really dreads going through his mom's things, though."

"That's probably what his obsession with getting the house cleaned up is really about."

"You may be right."

"Mm." Alicia tilted her head and narrowed her eyes at him. "Are you guys together yet? Exclusively, I mean?"

Paul laughed nervously. "Yeah, we are. I guess we've been exclusive for a while, really. We just finally made it official."

"Good!" She smiled, eyes shining. "I'm happy for you both."

"Thanks. I'm pretty happy myself." Paul returned her smile as he backed toward the door. "I better go finish mopping the kitchen."

Alicia chuckled. "Not anxious to get back home to Cory or anything, are you?"

"Maybe," Paul answered, flushing a little.

She sighed dramatically, one soapy hand pressed to her heart. "Ah, young love. So sweet."

Paul shook his head, laughing. "I'm gonna go finish the mopping, then get the bathroom cleaned."

"'Kay. That'll be it, then, right?"

"Right."

"Great. We'll have time to get the yard done before I have to go to work."

"Don't worry about that, I'll do it."

Alicia arched an eyebrow at him, then turned back to her scrubbing. Paul chuckled as he headed into the kitchen. Alicia's expression told him quite clearly that not only was she helping him with yard work whether he wanted her to or not, but she knew exactly why he was doing all this in the first place.

She was surprisingly perceptive, Paul thought. He couldn't deny that he still felt a twinge of guilt over what had happened the last time he'd been here. He knew Cory felt it too, though he hadn't said so. It was something they were both going to have to work through eventually.

As he worked, Paul's thoughts turned to the upcoming funeral. Mrs. Harrison had offered to help Cory make the arrangements. She'd shown up just before he left that morning to take Cory to the funeral home. Paul had come so close to asking Cory to let him pay for the funeral, but in the end he hadn't. He knew what Cory would say, especially now.

He ignored the little voice in the back of his mind which kept reminding him that this was another issue with the potential to push them apart. He was determined not to let that happen, no matter what.

⊞   ⊞   ⊞

A mouthwatering scent greeted Paul when he opened his front door that afternoon. He followed the heavenly aroma into the kitchen, where he found Mrs. Harrison stirring a large, fragrantly steaming pot.

"Mmmm." Paul threw the truck keys on the counter and leaned over the woman's shoulder. "What are you cooking? It smells great."

She smiled at him. "Hello, Paul. I made y'all some vegetable soup. Cory loves it." She stirred once more, put the lid on the pot, and cut the heat down. "Let it simmer another couple of hours, then you can eat it whenever you get hungry."

"Okay." Paul got a glass out of the cabinet and filled it with water. "You didn't have to do that. But I'm glad you did. Thanks."

"No trouble at all."

"Where's Cory?"

"Out back. Said he wanted to take a walk down to the river, and think." She wiped her hands on the kitchen towel and sat down at the table. "He didn't say so, but it was hard for him to have to pick a casket and all. Real hard."

Paul sat across from her, frowning at his glass of water. "This might not be the time to bring this up, but can he afford it? Funerals aren't cheap."

She gave him a considering look. "No, he can't. Not really. He's still paying off medical bills, and he's laid out a lot lately getting things fixed around the house. They gave him a pretty good deal on the casket, and helped him set up a payment plan. But they still need a down payment, and I don't know where Cory's gonna get that kind of money. I said I'd pay part, but he won't have it." She shook her head. "Stubbornest boy I ever knew."

"He sure is," Paul said wholeheartedly. "Don't suppose there's any use in me offering to help. Lord knows he's never let me before."

Mrs. Harrison reached across the table and took Paul's hand. "Give him some time. Our Cory's a proud boy, but he's smart, too. After he settles some, he'll realize that accepting your help won't make him any less in your eyes."

Paul smiled. He suspected that she'd hit Cory's biggest fear square on the head. "I hope you're right."

"Don't you worry. I've known Cory his whole life. He knows better than to let something good get away from him over a little thing like money." She squeezed Paul's hand, pushed her chair back, and stood. "I need to be off now. Y'all be sure to call me if you need anything."

"Okay." Paul stood and walked with her to the front door. "So what all arrangements did you make for the funeral?"

"The wake's tomorrow at three, at Thomlinson's Funeral Home. The funeral's Thursday morning at ten. I brought Cory's suit over; it's in your closet. Hope it still fits him. He hasn't worn it in a while."

"If it doesn't, I'll get him a new one." Paul put his arms around Mrs. Harrison in an impulsive hug. "Thank you."

"You're welcome." She patted his cheek, smiling as he let her go. "I'll see y'all tomorrow."

"All right."

He stood on the porch and watched her climb into her car, then waved as she pulled out of the driveway. The kitchen door banged shut just as he went back inside.

"Mrs. Harrison?" Cory called.

"She just left," Paul said, walking into the kitchen. "She made us some soup."

"Yeah, I can smell it." Cory went right into Paul's arms, snuggling against him. "I like this. Being here with you, I mean. It's nice just to know you're here. Makes me feel safe."

"I like it too." Paul leaned his cheek against Cory's salt-scented hair, feeling warm right down to his toes. "Is everything set for the funeral? Anything you need me to do?"

Cory tensed in Paul's arms. Paul held on, stroking his back and willing him to stay calm, stay relaxed. "No, it's all done." A short silence, then Cory whispered so low Paul could barely hear him. "Thank you. For taking care of my house."

"Alicia and I were happy to do it." Paul lifted Cory's chin and kissed him softly. "Anything you need me to do, I'll gladly do it."

"I know." A tear trickled down Cory's cheek. He brushed it away, mouth curving into a brave, tremulous smile that made Paul's heart ache. "Hey, when's the soup gonna be ready? Smells so good, it's making me hungry."

"Couple more hours, Mrs. Harrison said. Will cheese and crackers hold you 'til then? Maybe a beer?"

Cory nodded, the smile growing a little. Paul kissed him again, then pushed him down into a chair. "Sit. Crackers, cheese and beer coming right up."

Cory's eyes still looked lost and sorrowful, but Paul could see the tiny spark of happiness hiding deep inside, waiting for the hurt to ease so it could burst out. Just knowing that spark was there gave Paul a sense of hope.

There'd be tough times ahead, but Cory had the strength and the spirit to get through it. Paul vowed to be there to help him, every step of the way.

☒   ☒   ☒

So far, Cory had managed to avoid his mother's coffin. He kept catching glimpses of it on the far side of the room, a sinister presence in soft dove gray, surrounded by lilies and roses. Every time he saw the coffin, with Mama's head a vague, dark lump on the white pillow, he cut his eyes quickly away.

He really, really didn't want to see Mama lying in her coffin.

Cory closed his eyes and leaned against the high back of the antique chair. The afternoon sunlight poured through the many windows, glowing red against his closed eyelids. He still felt cold, though, in spite of the heavy suit jacket he wore. Thomlinson's Funeral Home was hardly a dreary place, but Cory had felt chilled to the marrow ever since he'd arrived for his mother's wake.

It had been less than three hours, but it seemed like years. He wondered if he'd ever be warm again.

Gentle fingers on his cheek startled his eyes open. Paul sat in the chair next to his, brow furrowed with worry. "You okay, Cory?"

Cory forced his frozen features into a smile. "Yeah. Just kind of tired."

He should've known Paul wouldn't be fooled. "If it's too hard to see her right now, that's okay. You don't have to."

Cory slipped his hand into Paul's. The long, elegant fingers wound protectively around his. "I can't." *I might break. I'm made of ice, and I might break.*

Paul stared hard at him. Those clear blue eyes seemed to see right into his core. "Let me take you home now."

Cory nodded and let Paul pull him to his feet. He imagined he could hear every joint in his frozen body popping in protest of the movement, every muscle screaming. He felt numb all over.

Paul made his way over to Mrs. Harrison, with Cory in tow. They spoke together in low tones for a minute. She hugged Cory and patted his cheek, but he couldn't hear what she said. His ears seemed to be stuffed with cotton. Mrs. Harrison and Paul exchanged a worried look which he knew must be about him, but the cold inside him had crept into his brain and he couldn't find the energy to care. He turned, scanning the room. A flash of polished gray hit his eyes, framing a face whiter than the lilies, and everything went blank.

Sitting in the front seat of the truck on the way to Paul's house, Cory stared out the window and tried to recall how he'd gotten there. Paul must've made his excuses to the crowd that had shown up for the wake, but he couldn't remember it. He remembered standing beside Mrs. Harrison, turning to find himself face-to-face with the open casket, then the scene abruptly shifted and he was in the truck with Paul. He could feel the blank space between seeing his mother's face and being buckled into Paul's truck, but his mind couldn't fill it. He watched the sunny August afternoon go by outside and wondered idly if he was going crazy.

Paul didn't say a word the whole trip. By the time they reached Paul's house a hard lump of dread had formed in Cory's guts. What if Paul was angry with him? The idea ballooned until it was all he could think of.

Paul parked the truck in front of the house, just like he'd done the day Mama died, so that Cory wouldn't have far to walk. *Such a sweet thing to do. Everything he does is sweet.*

When Paul took his hand to lead him into the house, Cory stopped, staring into Paul's eyes. "I'm sorry, Paul."

"What for?" Paul's face radiated surprise.

"For freaking out," Cory whispered. "I, I don't know what I did, I can't remember."

"Oh, baby, no." Paul pulled Cory into his arms. "You didn't do anything wrong, okay? I was telling Mrs. Harrison I was taking you home, you turned around and saw your mother, and...you sort of blanked out. You just stood there, staring at your mom. So I got you out of there as fast as I could."

"Shit." Cory wound both arms around Paul's waist and rested his head on Paul's shoulder. "Everybody must think I'm nuts."

"Actually, I don't think anyone noticed, other than Mrs. Harrison and me."

"Good." Cory snuggled closer, nuzzling Paul's neck. "So I didn't embarrass you?"

"No." Paul kissed Cory's head, hands stroking down his back. "Scared me a little."

"Sorry."

"Don't be." Paul pulled back, keeping one arm around Cory's shoulders. "Now come on, let's go in."

Cory followed Paul inside and into the bedroom. Paul helped him undress, then tucked him into bed as if he were a child. Cory didn't argue, just let Paul take care of him. When Paul kissed his brow and turned to walk away, Cory clutched at his hand.

"Don't leave me," Cory heard himself plead.

Paul sat on the bed. One hand combed soothingly through Cory's hair. "Want to talk?"

Cory stared up into Paul's eyes, trying to find the words. "I can't feel anything, Paul. I know I should. But I just can't."

Paul smiled sadly at him. "I guess you can't always feel the way you have the past couple of days. It's too much."

Cory wanted to cry, but the tears wouldn't come. The grief and anger and terror were buried too deep inside him, locked away by the strange wall of ice. He took Paul's hand and laid the palm against his bare belly. He wasn't sure why, except that he simply needed to be touched. Paul's eyes filled with heat and need. Cory could tell he was trying to hide it, but it wasn't working.

"Come to bed." Cory pulled Paul's face down and kissed him hard. "I need you."

Paul's hands shook violently. Whether with desire or with horror at himself for feeling it, Cory couldn't tell. Right then, he didn't really care. He just needed to feel something, anything.

"Cory..." Paul's voice was rough. "God. Are...are you..."

"I don't know. I don't know anything right now. I just...just need you." Cory squeezed his eyes shut, arms tight around Paul's neck, holding him down. "Please, Paul, please."

Paul made a soft, hungry sound when Cory kissed him again. Cory let Paul go long enough for him to get undressed, then lifted the covers and pulled Paul to him. Cory wound himself vine-like around Paul's body, seeking the warmth of his bare skin and soft, wet mouth.

It didn't take Cory long to figure out that it wasn't going to happen. Panic edged bright and sharp on the outskirts of his mind when he realized that his body wasn't responding to Paul's touch. Even that wasn't enough to shatter the ice that held him in its grip.

He felt Paul's erection wilting against his thigh, and wished he could sink right through the floor. He unwrapped himself from Paul's body and turned away, curled into a ball, face buried in his hands.

After a moment, the mattress shifted. Paul molded himself to Cory's back, arms snugly around his waist. "It's okay," he whispered in Cory's ear. "It's not the right time."

Cory let himself relax into Paul's embrace. "I just wanted to feel alive again."

"I know, baby." Paul kissed his neck, wound the fingers of one hand through Cory's. "I know."

Cory curled up tighter, holding Paul around him like a blanket. "I'm so fucking cold."

Paul pulled the covers up over them both, then tucked his arm around Cory's waist again, one leg thrown over Cory's hips. "Rest now."

"You'll stay?"

"I'm not going anywhere."

Cory sighed and closed his eyes. Secure in the knowledge of Paul's presence, he slept.

CHAPTER THIRTEEN

Paul shut the door on the last visitor with a grateful sigh. Much as he appreciated all the food and offers of help from the townspeople, the constant stream of visitors had worn him out.

"You've got four green bean casseroles, two platters of fried chicken, a pot roast, five different kinds of salad, and a pot of corn on the cob," Alicia said, wandering in from the kitchen. "And I made some iced tea."

"Thanks." Paul gave her a tired smile. "I still can't get over how many people have brought food over. Funerals aren't like this back home."

And just like that, Paul's mind flew back to the funeral he'd never had the chance to attend. The first one to ever truly matter to him, and he'd missed it.

Paul's throat tightened at the sudden memory. Alicia narrowed her eyes at him. "Paul? You all right?"

"I lost my partner just over a year ago. The funeral sort of brought it all back." Paul took a deep breath, trying to keep his voice from shaking. "I was in the hospital when they buried him."

Alicia's sharp gaze softened. "I'm sorry."

"I miss him." Paul blinked back the tears that threatened, and managed a smile. "But we were together for six years, and those were damn good years. And I have Cory now. I think I'm pretty damn lucky."

Alicia took both of Paul's hands in hers, stood on tiptoe, and kissed his cheek. "You're a good man, Paul. I'm glad Cory has you. Especially right now."

"I'd have to agree," Mrs. Harrison said, coming in from the bathroom. "That boy's just like a son to me. It eases my mind, knowing you're looking after him."

"Where'd he go?" Alicia asked, frowning. "I need to go, I wanted to say goodbye."

"Same here," Mrs. Harrison said.

"In the bedroom to change," Paul said. "I'll go tell him you guys are leaving."

Paul went down the hall and tapped on the closed bedroom door. "Cory, you decent? Alicia and Mrs. Harrison have to leave. They want to say goodbye."

No answer. Apprehensive now, Paul turned the knob and pushed the door open. Cory was curled up sound asleep in the armchair, wearing only gray boxer-briefs and his unbuttoned dress shirt, head pillowed on his arm. Paul smiled and shut the door.

"He's asleep," Paul said as he walked back into the living room. "Sorry."

Mrs. Harrison smiled. "Well, let him sleep. I guess he's probably worn right out."

"Yeah. Been a rough few days." Paul decided not to mention Cory's strange, blank mood since the wake the previous day. They'd only worry, and they couldn't do a damn thing to help. Paul knew from experience that it would pass eventually. But in the meantime, nothing anyone said or did would make any difference.

"Okay, I'm off." Alicia hugged Paul hard. "Tell Cory we said bye, and we love him."

"Sure." Paul squeezed her hand. "Thanks for everything, Alicia. You too, Mrs. Harrison. Don't know what Cory and I would've done the last few days without you both."

Mrs. Harrison hugged Paul and gently patted his cheek. "Y'all are family, Paul. Families look after each other."

Paul's eyes stung. He nodded, not trusting his voice. Mrs. Harrison and Alicia left, making him promise to call if he and Cory needed anything. After they'd gone, Paul went back to the bedroom and stood leaning against the wall, watching Cory sleep. He looked so sweet and untroubled, the sight pulled Paul like a magnet. Unable to resist, he moved quietly over to the chair, leaned down, and softly kissed Cory's cheek.

Cory stirred. Green eyes fluttered open. "Hey, Paul," he mumbled sleepily.

He held his arms up. Paul scooped him up, sat down in the chair, and settled Cory on his lap. "Hey, sleepyhead."

Cory cuddled against Paul's chest, arms around his neck, tousled curls pressed to Paul's cheek. "Is everyone gone?"

"Yeah. Alicia and Mrs. Harrison just left. They said to tell you they love you, and to call if you need them."

"Didn't mean to fall asleep. Sorry."

173

"Don't worry about it. Most everybody had gone anyway when you came in here. I was just talking to the Hathaways from down the road, they were the last."

"They're nice folks."

"Sure are. They asked if I'd do a portrait of their grandchildren."

"Oh, yeah?"

"Mm-hm. It's funny, a lot of people asked about my painting. I don't remember telling anyone other than you, but it seems like everyone knows I was an artist."

"*Are* an artist," Cory corrected. "It's a small town. Word gets around. You gonna do it?"

"I think so. It'll be nice to work again." Paul shifted so that he could see Cory's face. "How do you feel, Cory? I know the funeral was hard."

Cory's eyes clouded. "I'm just glad it's over. It was fucking awful, Paul."

Paul held Cory tighter. "I'm sorry, baby."

"I could've handled burying her if it was just us, you know? You and me. It would've still been hard, but I could've handled it, I think. But all those fucking people, I know most of them knew Mama and they wanted to say goodbye too, but I just felt..." Cory stopped, brow creased. When he spoke again, his voice had dropped to a near whisper. "I felt like they were all watching me, you know, just waiting for me to break down so they could feel sorry for me. I know they weren't really, but it felt like it anyway. I fucking hated it."

"It's over now, Cory." Paul threaded a hand into Cory's hair and leaned their foreheads together. "It's just the two of us, and you know you don't have to hide anything from me."

"I know." Cory's fingers traced the line of Paul's jaw. "Kiss me."

Paul happily complied. The kiss went deep, sweet and soft and unhurried. Paul felt their mutual desire simmering under the surface, but there was no urgency to it. When they pulled apart at last and Cory rested his head in the curve of Paul's neck, Paul thought it was one of the most peaceful moments of his life.

※　※　※

The remainder of the day was spent doing nothing much. Paul and Cory walked across the meadow and down to the river, strolling barefoot along the strip of sand that ran beside it. They followed the river's meandering path all the way to where it emptied into the Atlantic, and walked hand in hand down the beach for a while. The waves washed blood-warm against Paul's bare legs. A cool breeze tossed their hair and dampened the heat of the afternoon sun.

By the time they returned home, the brilliant blue of the sky had hazed over and the wind had turned keen, howling around the corners of the house. A few minutes later, sullen black clouds rolled in, accompanied by ominous peals of thunder. Paul and Cory stood on the back porch and watched the lightning flash in the gloom, making the grass and trees glow strangely. When the first fat raindrops gave way to a blinding downpour, they went back inside, curled up on the bed together, and fell asleep in each other's arms.

Paul woke abruptly when the phone rang. Stumbling out of bed to answer it, he glanced at the clock. They'd slept for about two hours.

He ran into the kitchen and snatched the phone up on the fifth ring, thinking he really had to put an extension in the bedroom. "Hello?"

"Hi, is this Paul Gordon?"

"Yes, it is."

"Mr. Gordon, I'm Jenny Thomlinson, from the funeral home. Cory said we could reach him at your home, is he available?"

"He's sleeping," Paul answered, trying hard to keep the irritation out of his voice. "It's been a difficult day for him."

"Yes, of course." The woman on the other end sounded hesitant. "Well, if you could just tell him to call when he gets a moment, I'd appreciate it."

"Paul? Is that for me?"

Paul turned around. Cory shuffled over to him, yawning, and leaned on his shoulder. "Yes, it's the funeral home," Paul said, covering the mouthpiece with one hand. "You don't have to talk right now, I told them you were asleep."

"Naw, it's okay." Cory took the phone before Paul could object. "Hi, this is Cory."

Cory turned away and walked into the living room, obviously seeking privacy. Paul didn't follow, even though he wanted to. Instead, he peered out the screen door into the cool, damp evening. The storm had settled into a gentle rain that pattered on the grass and the roof. The rays of the setting sun shone from under a ragged edge of cloud, turning the falling raindrops into a sparkling silver curtain.

"Yes, I know." Cory's voice floated from the living room, sounding stressed. Paul strained to hear in spite of himself. "I'll get it to you as soon as possible, but... Yes... I know, and I appreciate that, really, but I just don't have it right now... I know... Okay, I have about a hundred and fifty at my house, I can bring it to you tomorrow... I know, but that's every dime I've got right now. I can't give you what I don't have."

Cory's voice dropped down low and Paul lost the thread of the conversation. But he'd heard enough to know what it was about: the down payment Cory owed for his mother's funeral. *What kind of people are they,* he thought heatedly, *to call a man for money on the day he buries his mother?*

Paul forced himself to smile when Cory came back into the kitchen to hang up the phone. "So, what'd they want?" he asked, pulling Cory into his arms and kissing his forehead.

Cory sighed. "I owe them five hundred dollars. They set up a payment plan for me, so I could pay off the rest in installments, but they need the five hundred right away."

It was all Paul could do to keep his voice calm. "Surely they can wait a while, huh? They have to know you don't exactly have that kind of money lying around. Not many people do."

"They've already made an exception for me, Paul. Normally they want payment up front, in full. They let me wait until after the funeral, and they're letting me pay on the balance monthly. I can't ask them to do more than that."

"Where're you gonna get five hundred dollars?"

Cory was silent for so long that Paul didn't think he was going to answer. "I don't have a fucking clue," he said finally. "It'll take me a while to earn that much, even working extra shifts and without the usual expenses..."

Cory's voice broke. Paul held him close, trying not to notice the way his breath hitched as if he were fighting not to cry.

Paul knew what he wanted to say, and he knew it was a bad idea before he ever opened his mouth. But he had to say it.

"I can help," he murmured against Cory's ear. "Let me pay it. The five hundred at least. Please."

Cory tensed against him, palms flat on Paul's chest as if he meant to push away. Paul's arms tightened, refusing to let him go. "Cory, please let me do this for you. There's no need for you to work double shifts and struggle to come up with that money, when I can write them a check right now."

Cory went completely still, staring at Paul with shock written all over his face. *Oh, shit,* Paul thought. He barely had time to brace himself before Cory's eyes went dark and he shoved Paul away hard.

"Who the *fuck* do you think you are, huh?" Cory's voice was shaking. "I told you before, I don't need your fucking money. I can take care of myself."

"I know that," Paul said, keeping his voice deliberately calm. "And I know we've been over this ground before. I just want to help, that's all."

"I don't want to be your fucking charity project!"

"You're not." Paul reached out and touched Cory's cheek, looking deep into his angry, pain-filled eyes. "We love each other, Cory. Can't you trust me to do this for the right reasons?"

Cory stared back. He looked like he was about to say something. But he didn't. Shaking his head, Cory backed away, turned, and strode out the back door.

Paul wanted to follow, but he didn't. Much as it hurt to have Cory angry with him, he knew the anger wasn't truly directed at him. He'd felt that same anger after Jay died. A deep, unfocused fury looking for a direction. If Cory needed an outlet, Paul would gladly be that for him. He could handle that a lot better than the strange, icy calm Cory had lived in since the wake. His relief at seeing emotions breaking through that unnatural calm almost negated the hurt of arguing with Cory today of all days.

Paul gazed out the window at Cory pacing through the grass, hands in his pockets, clothes and hair damp with the lingering rain. Ignoring the urge to run out the door and sweep Cory into his arms, Paul turned away and started fixing dinner.

🔳　🔳　🔳

Soothed by the growing gloom under the trees, by the fireflies and crickets and the cool drizzle, Cory's anger drained away as suddenly as it had arisen. He didn't know why he'd said what he'd said. Paul sure as hell didn't deserve the accusations he'd hurled at him. Especially since he *did* trust Paul, more deeply than he'd ever trusted anyone.

Cory stopped pacing the backyard and gazed into the kitchen window. He could see Paul moving around inside. Taking plates from the cabinet, food from the refrigerator, setting the table. Light spilled from the window across the darkened yard, warm and inviting. For one bright second, Cory pictured himself in there beside Paul, the two of them laughing and stealing kisses as they worked. Right then, Cory wanted that comfortable domesticity so badly that it was almost a physical ache.

Maybe we can have that, Paul and me. Maybe we can.

It wasn't long before Paul caught him staring. Those pale blue eyes stared back, Paul smiled, and just like that Cory knew it would all be okay. The burning in his throat eased a little, and he returned Paul's smile.

Paul swung the screen door open and strolled across the yard to stand beside Cory. They walked to the edge of the trees, fingers winding together.

"Dinner's ready, if you're hungry," Paul said, nudging Cory's shoulder with his.

"Yeah, I am. Thanks."

They stood in silence for a while, watching the mist rise from the river, ghostlike in the gathering dark. The edge of the sky glowed deep red behind the pines. Cory leaned his head on Paul's shoulder, and Paul rested his cheek against Cory's hair.

"Paul?"

"Hm?"

"I didn't mean any of that. And I do trust you."

"I know."

Silence again. A whippoorwill added its mournful tones to the rising chorus of bullfrogs and crickets.

Gathering all his courage, Cory clasped Paul's hand tight and told him just how much he trusted him. "If you still want to, I could sure use your help paying for Mama's funeral."

Cory could hear Paul's smile in his voice. "Yeah, I still want to."

With darkness around them and dinner waiting inside, they kissed once and headed back into the kitchen. Cory didn't try to stop the tears from falling when the green bean casserole brought back memories of his mother's cooking. Paul didn't seem to mind at all, just sat beside Cory with an arm around his shoulders and listened to him talk about the good times with Mama. It felt good to be able to talk and cry, to have someone to share it all with.

It felt good to be warm and alive again.

When Cory looked into Paul's eyes, he saw his future. And for the first time in a long, long time, that future shone bright as the summer sun.

CHAPTER FOURTEEN

Cory found it strange sometimes that the day-to-day details of his life remained essentially unchanged when its bedrock had shifted so drastically. His mother was gone, he'd practically moved in with Paul, and he hadn't been to work in nearly a month. Yet he still slept and ate and talked to people and even laughed sometimes, just as if nothing had changed.

Maybe, he thought, that's how you stay sane when life throws you a curve.

"Cory?"

Cory blinked, and turned to look at Paul. "Uh, sorry, I kind of zoned out."

"It's okay." Paul pulled him close. "You sure you're ready for this?"

"Yeah. I'm ready." Cory slipped both arms around Paul's waist. "It's been three weeks. I need to get this over with."

Paul pressed a gentle kiss to Cory's lips. "You need to leave, let me know, okay?"

"Sure."

Paul kissed him again and started toward the house, one hand still linked with his. Cory followed, trying to ignore the way his legs shook. Paul unlocked the door, and Cory held his breath as they stepped inside the house where he'd spent his whole life.

It looked the same as ever. The stained and cracked linoleum, the worn furniture, the big purple stain on the living room carpet where he'd spilled grape juice when he was ten. Cory almost expected Mama to come out of the bedroom in her blue scrubs, ready for work. His throat went tight.

"Paul. Paul, wait." Cory stopped, clutching Paul's hand hard. "Wait a minute."

Paul touched Cory's cheek. "You can go through your mom's things any time. It doesn't have to be now."

"No, I want to do it now. It's just…" Cory closed his eyes and leaned against Paul's chest. "It's just hard, you know?"

"Yeah. I know." Paul's voice was soft and sad. "Wish I could make it easier."

"You're here, Paul. That makes it easier."

"Good."

Cory opened his eyes and looked up into Paul's. They moved forward at the same time, mouths meeting in a deep kiss. Paul cradled the back of Cory's skull in one hand and slid the other around his waist. Desire fluttered in Cory's belly, maddeningly elusive, just strong enough to make him long for more even as his body refused to respond. He let out a frustrated whimper, fingers digging into Paul's sides.

Paul broke the kiss, his breathing fast and ragged. "Sorry. This isn't the time, I shouldn't have—"

"You didn't. We both did." Cory stroked the soft dark hair from Paul's brow, wishing he could explain how he felt. "I want you so much, Paul. But I can't. Not yet. I don't know why."

Paul's smile was sad. "I don't think sex would be on most people's minds at a time like this, Cory."

"I just want to feel normal again."

"You will. It just takes a little time, that's all."

Cory brushed a finger gently over Paul's lower lip, loving the way his eyes hazed at the touch. "I miss making love with you."

Paul let out a soft, needy sound. "Me too."

"I'm sorry."

"Don't." Paul framed Cory's face in both hands. "I love you, Cory. I'll be with you through everything you're going through right now, and I'll be right here when you're ready for sex again. There's no hurry. I'm not going anywhere."

A sharp, sweet warmth bloomed in Cory's chest, so intense it was almost painful. He smiled through the tears that were suddenly spilling down his face.

"Paul," he whispered, his voice cracked and shaking and barely audible. "I love you. I do."

There was so much more he wanted to say, but the words wouldn't come. Looking into Paul's soft blue eyes, though, Cory was sure he understood. He rested his head in the curve of Paul's neck, and Paul held him while he cried.

The past three weeks had taught Cory exactly how cathartic tears could be. He'd lost track of how many times he'd sobbed in Paul's arms since Mama's funeral. Painful as the stabbing grief was, allowing himself to feel it wore away some of its sharpness each time. These storms always left him feeling drained, but peaceful.

By the time his tears tapered off, Cory felt calm enough to face the task of sorting through the memories of his mother's life. With Paul beside him, he thought he might just be strong enough to do it.

Paul smiled at him, brushing a few lingering tears off his cheeks. "You okay?"

Cory nodded, wiping his nose on the tissue Paul handed him. "Yeah. I'm ready now."

After a moment's thought, Cory decided to start in Mama's bedroom. His gut told him that room would be the hardest to face, so he wanted to do it right away, while he still felt calm and centered. He didn't mention his reasons, but Paul squeezed his hand as if he knew.

It took surprisingly little time to sort through the dresser drawers and the tiny closet. Cory gazed at the clothing and personal possessions he and Paul had piled onto the bare box spring, thinking how pitifully small the little pile was. He'd always known that Mama had never bought much for herself, preferring to spend what little extra money she had on things for the house, or for Cory. Seeing how few possessions she'd left behind brought that fact home to him, along with a sharp pang of regret for all the things she'd never had.

Paul's arms wrapping around him from behind brought him out of his thoughts. He turned his head and pulled Paul's face to his for a kiss.

"What're you thinking about?" Paul asked as Cory drew back again.

"Just that Mama never had as much as she deserved. I wish I could've changed that."

Paul nuzzled his hair. "She had you. That's better than all the clothes and money in the world."

Cory didn't answer, but he knew Paul was right, and that was a comfort.

The bathroom was next. Cory threw out everything except the soap and shampoo in the shower. Paul had brought Cory's other things to his house long ago. After the bathroom, they bypassed the kitchen and started on the shelves that covered one whole wall of the living room. Outdated magazines, a broken alarm clock, and a plastic vase of faded silk flowers went into the big trash bag. The books Cory and his mother had collected over the years stayed where they were, filling all but a few of the shelves.

Cory was dusting the newly emptied shelves when Paul let out a soft gasp. "Oh, Cory. Come here."

Cory reluctantly set down the cloth he'd been dusting with and went to join Paul. "What'd you find?" he asked, even though he already knew.

Paul smiled at him from where he sat on the floor. "Pictures. Several albums full. Did you know these were here?"

"Yeah. I used to look at them a lot when Mama first got sick."

Paul reached up and took his hand. "You want to look at them now?"

Cory shook his head, more violently than he'd intended to. "No. Not now."

"Okay." Paul set down the album in his hand and rose gracefully to his feet, still holding Cory's hand. "Want to bring them home with us? That way they'll be right there for you to look at whenever you want."

"Sure." Cory gave Paul a shaky smile. "Thanks, Paul. For understanding me. I don't think anybody else could."

"I've been where you are, not so long ago. It took me a month to work up the courage to go through Jay's things, and nearly three months until I could look at his picture without breaking down." Paul laid a hand on Cory's cheek. "It *will* get better, Cory. I promise it will. Healing takes time, and you have to give yourself that time."

Cory didn't say a word, just put his arms around Paul's neck and hugged him close.

🂠　🂠　🂠

In the end, it only took another week for Cory to open the photo albums. He and Paul sat side by side on the sofa on a warm September evening, Cory's head resting on Paul's shoulder as they made their way through the pages of fading photos. Cory shed a few tears, but he also smiled and laughed, and related endless tales of the small-town adventures he and his mother had shared. It made Paul happy to hear those stories, and to see how Cory's eyes lit up with the memories.

"Wow, Cory," Paul said, chuckling over a picture of an eleven-year-old Cory and his mother dressed up as zombies for Halloween. "Looks like you and your mom had lots of fun."

"We did." Cory sounded wistful, but content. "She was the best mom in the world."

Paul lifted Cory's chin and kissed him lightly on the lips. "Thanks for showing me these. I love them."

Cory smiled. "I'm glad you were here to look at them with me. I'm not sure I could've done it alone."

"Bet you could." Paul raked a hand through Cory's curls. "But I'm glad you didn't have to."

"You're so good to me, Paul." Cory leaned forward and kissed Paul's chin, then his lower lip. "I'm a lucky guy."

Paul stared into Cory's eyes from inches away. They were emerald bright and full of need. Paul took the photo album from Cory's hands, set it on the coffee table, and pulled Cory to him.

After more than a month of deprivation, gentle kisses quickly turned heated, soft tentative touches became rough and demanding. Cory's breathless whimpers set Paul's brain on fire. Cory ripped Paul's shirt open, sending buttons pattering to the floor. Paul wriggled out of the shirt and tossed it over the back of the sofa.

"Paul. Paul, please." Cory's teeth dug into Paul's earlobe. Paul could practically smell his desire. "Want you, now, right now."

Paul's voice refused to work, but he figured it didn't matter. If his need was as transparent as Cory's, words wouldn't be necessary.

He fell back onto the sofa, pulling Cory on top of him. "Off," he gasped, fumbling frantically at Cory's shorts.

Cory squirmed the cutoffs down his thighs and tugged one leg free, leaving the shorts tangled around one ankle, then yanked his T-shirt off. Sprawled naked between Paul's legs, he went still, green eyes hot and wild.

"Want to be inside you," Cory whispered hoarsely.

The thought of it made Paul burn. "Yeah. Fuck me."

Working together, they managed to get Paul's shorts off between kisses. Cory wet two fingers in his mouth and pushed them both roughly into Paul's ass. Paul gasped, legs falling wide open, knees drawing up to give Cory better access. Cory crooked his fingers just so, and Paul saw stars. Cory let out a soft little moan.

"Paul, please, I need...I need..."

"'S okay," Paul panted. "Do it."

Cory spit into his palm, slicked his cock, and penetrated Paul in one swift stroke. Paul cried out, hips lifting to take Cory in all the way. It hurt, but he wanted it, needed the burning pain that melted into an ecstasy big enough to swallow the world. He buried both hands in Cory's hair and pulled him into a fierce kiss.

"Oh," Cory breathed against Paul's lips. "Fuck, so tight."

Paul let out a strained laugh. "Been a while. Oh, oh God, right there, yeah!"

Cory angled up again, hitting that spot that set off explosions in Paul's body, and Paul lost what little control he had left. He wrapped his legs around Cory's waist and hung on, fingers digging into Cory's back hard enough to bruise. He heard himself as if from a great distance, begging Cory to fuck him harder, telling him in broken half-formed phrases how much he wanted Cory inside him forever. His voice sounded rough and wanton, and he liked that, liked being able to give Cory all of himself.

"Fuck, gonna come." Cory's voice was tight, his arms trembling against Paul's ribs.

"Come on. Come in my ass."

Cory's eyes fluttered closed. His hips slammed against Paul's ass over and over, driving his prick in deep, until he came with a shudder and a cry. The look on his face, soft and rapturous, sent Paul spiraling over the edge. He clung to Cory like a lifeline as the orgasm swept over him, hot and sweet and overpowering.

"Oh. Oh, wow." Cory collapsed onto Paul's chest, breathing hard. "God, that was so damn good."

"Mmm. I like having you inside me."

"I like it too." Cory raised his head, smiling. "Kiss me."

Paul happily obeyed. He ran his palms down Cory's bare back as they kissed. Cory's skin was so soft beneath his hands, soft and warm and damp with sweat. He could feel Cory's heart beating against his chest.

Cory moaned when Paul's finger brushed his hole. "Paul?"

"Yeah?" He bit Cory's neck.

"Let's take a shower."

"What?" Paul laughed.

Cory grinned at him. "We're gonna be stuck together permanently if we don't wash off pretty soon."

"I don't mind being stuck to you." Paul clamped down hard on Cory's cock, which was already swelling inside him, and Cory gasped.

"But there's so many things we could do in the shower."

"True." Paul pushed on Cory's chest. "Okay, you talked me into it. Let's go."

"Yeah." Cory eased out of Paul, biting his lip as he slid free. He stood, swaying a little, and pulled Paul to his feet. "You do me this time."

"Whatever you say." Paul nipped Cory's ear, making him squeal. "C'mon."

They stumbled toward the bathroom, arms around each other and mouths locked together. Paul barely noticed when he banged his shin on the coffee table. In the bathroom, Cory broke the kiss long enough to turn on the shower. They stepped under the warm spray together, already kissing again.

"God, Paul." Cory licked Paul's throat. "Want you so bad."

"Mmm." Paul slid his hands down to cup Cory's ass, squeezing gently. "Turn around, baby."

"Why?" Cory slid a knee between Paul's legs. "What're you gonna do?"

Paul groaned, rocking against Cory's thigh. "Gonna open you up with my tongue."

Cory's cheeks went pink. "Oh, hell yeah." He wrapped a hand around Paul's shaft, eyes blazing. "Will you stick this in me, once you've got me all loose and begging for it?"

"Better believe it. Now turn around."

Cory obediently turned to face the wall. He gave Paul a smoldering look over his shoulder. Paul molded himself to Cory's back, letting his erection nestle between Cory's buttocks. He slid both hands down Cory's arms, lacing their fingers together. The warm water pounding down his back seemed unbearably sensual, the rising steam scented with semen and sweat and desire.

"Put your hands on the wall." Paul raised their joined hands and planted Cory's palms against the tiles. "And spread your legs."

Cory slid his feet apart. His fingers curled against the porcelain. "Hurry."

Paul bent to kiss Cory's neck. "Relax," he whispered. "I want to take my time." He trailed his fingertips down Cory's sides. The soft golden skin jumped and shivered under his touch. "Want to taste every inch of you."

He flicked his tongue over the place where Cory's neck curved into his shoulder, then latched on and sucked hard. Cory arched against him. "Oh, oh God!"

Paul leaned down to bite at the hollow behind Cory's left shoulder blade, hands mapping the curve of hip and thigh. Cory let out a desperate wail when Paul's fingers gently brushed his balls. The sound went straight to Paul's cock. It was all he could do to resist shoving his dick up Cory's ass right then. He squeezed the tip of Cory's cock between his thumb and forefinger, just to hear those wonderfully needy sounds again.

"Paul, God please, please..." Cory's voice shook almost as hard as his body. "I need you."

"You've got me, Cory." Paul sank slowly to his knees, planting soft little kisses down Cory's spine. "Christ, you make the most amazing noises."

Cory's breathless laugh morphed into a hoarse cry when Paul spread him open and circled his hole with the tip of his tongue. "Fuck, fuck yes! Don't stop!"

Paul didn't answer, his mouth being occupied with something far better than words. Cory smelled like sex and tasted even better. Paul heard his own needy moans blending with Cory's sharp cries. It excited him that he could make Cory sound like that.

He licked and probed until the tight little hole began to open for him. Cory keened and pushed back against him as he plunged his tongue in deep, over and over again. "Oh God! Paul please, please fuck me, I need it!"

Molten heat pooled in Paul's belly at the sound of those panting, husky pleas, and that was all he could stand. He stood and shoved his prick up Cory's ass in one motion.

Cory gasped. He leaned forward, head hanging down and hands scrabbling at the tiles. "Oh...yes..."

Paul leaned across Cory's back, one hand on the wall, the other reaching down to grasp Cory's shaft. A violent shudder ran through Cory's body, causing his insides to ripple and clench around Paul's cock. Paul moaned. "God, you feel so good."

Cory was silent, breath coming in ragged gulps. Paul knew he was close. The tension in his body spoke volumes. Letting his restraint go, Paul took Cory hard, roughly stroking the hard prick in his hand as he pounded into Cory's body. When he came, everything went eerily silent, a white haze clouding his vision. He couldn't hear Cory's wild cry as he came on Paul's hand, but he felt it, just as he felt Cory's body shaking against his. He buried his face in the curve of Cory's neck and wished he could stop time right there.

As soon as he could move again, Paul pulled out of Cory and gently turned him around. Cory melted into his arms. They shared a long, lazy kiss. When it ended, Cory smiled at him, green eyes glowing with content.

"Paul, have I told you lately that you're a great lay?"

Paul laughed. "Glad you think so. I could say the same." He cupped Cory's face in his hands. "You look so happy right now."

"I am. I feel like the worst is over now, you know? Like everything really is gonna be okay."

"So, you're all right? It wasn't too soon?"

"It was just in time." Cory worked his fingers through Paul's wet hair. "I'll always miss her. She's my mother and I love her. But I'm fine now." He pulled Paul closer and gently kissed his lips. "I don't think I would've made it without you, Paul."

Something tightened in Paul's chest. He started to speak, then yelped as the shower suddenly ran cold. Laughing, Cory reached back to shut the water off.

Paul grabbed a towel off the rack and handed it to Cory, then grabbed another for himself. "Guess we stayed in too long."

Cory gave him a wicked grin as they stepped out onto the bathmat. "It was worth it."

Paul stopped drying his hair and stared hard at Cory. He didn't know if he should ask or not, but he heard himself speaking the words anyway. "Move in with me, Cory."

Cory raised an eyebrow at him. "In case you didn't notice, I've been staying here for the past month."

"I know." Paul laid a hand on Cory's cheek. "Maybe this is the wrong time to say this, but I don't want you to leave. I want us to live together. Permanently."

For an endless second, Cory stared back at him, wide-eyed and silent. Then he smiled, and Paul's heart started beating again. "I'd love that."

Paul thought it might be the happiest moment of his life. He tugged on Cory's hand. Cory came to him, and they kissed for a long time. When the kiss ended, Cory laid his head on Paul's shoulder.

Holding Cory warm and naked in his arms, Paul thought of Jay. The love they'd shared, the life they'd made together. When Jay died, Paul hadn't thought he'd survive it. But he *had* survived. And now, he had Cory. A second chance at love. Paul rested his cheek against Cory's hair and smiled.

EPILOGUE

"Paul, do you think she'll like this wine?" Cory frowned at the bottle of Chianti in his hand. "This isn't good enough. I'll go to town and get something else."

Laughing, Paul grabbed Cory's arm before he could get to the kitchen door. "This one's fine. Everything's fine. Stop worrying."

Cory slipped his arms around Paul's waist. "I just want to make a good impression. I want your mom to like me."

"She's going to love you." Paul lifted Cory's chin and pressed a light kiss to his lips. "Just settle down, huh?"

"I can't help being nervous." Cory bit his lip. "What if she's mad about Christmas?"

Paul's parents had invited both of them to spend the holidays in Spokane. Paul was the one who'd turned down the invitation, saying that he didn't feel up to making the long trip, but Cory knew the real reason. He hadn't felt ready to face anyone else, to have to hide his inevitable bouts of sadness. He'd never said so, but Paul knew. Paul could read him like a book. So they'd put up a tree in the living room and spent the day talking. He'd cried a little, missing Mama, but mostly it had been good. Happy. The only thing that marred it for him was a nagging guilt for keeping Paul and his family apart on Christmas. He couldn't quite believe that Paul's mother wouldn't resent him for it.

"She's not mad," Paul said softly. "She understands, believe me."

Cory nodded and managed a smile. "Okay. If you say so."

"I do say so." Paul kissed Cory again, deeper this time. "I better go. Mom's plane's due in at six-fifteen."

Cory glanced at the clock. "You've got nearly an hour. It won't take that long to get to the airport."

Paul grinned in that way that said he knew exactly what Cory wanted. "Think we have time?"

"Mm-hm." Cory rolled his hips against Paul's, loving the feel of Paul's growing hardness against his own. "I just put the veal parmesan in the oven, and you've got at least ten minutes before you have to go. We have time for a quickie."

Paul's eyes hazed over. Winding a hand into Cory's hair, he kissed him hard and deep, his free hand expertly working Cory's jeans open. Cory did the same, flipping open the button of Paul's jeans and tugging the zipper down without looking. They let out identical lustful moans when their cocks touched.

Cory broke the kiss to look down at his and Paul's hands intertwined around their two shafts. The sight made him ache. He leaned his forehead against Paul's and watched them stroke each other, fast and rough. He felt dizzy and breathless, drowning in sensation, his entire body electrified. It was always like that with Paul. Like every time was the first. He never got over the wonder of it.

"Oh God," Paul breathed, and came hard. A drop of warm semen landed on Cory's lip. He licked it off. Already teetering on the brink, the taste sent him tumbling. His release roared through him, and his knees buckled as he came.

"Wow." Cory leaned against Paul's chest, letting Paul hold him up. "I needed that."

Paul laughed. "Will you relax now, you think?"

"Uh-huh." Cory gave Paul a lazy smile. "Hey, you realize this is how we started, right?"

"Like I could forget."

"Been nine months. Almost to the day."

"Doesn't seem like that long."

"Nope."

Paul reached for the dishtowel lying crumpled on the counter and started wiping the semen off their hands and clothes. Those pale blue eyes searched Cory's, serious and intent. "Are you happy, Cory?"

"Happier than I ever thought I could be." Cory drew Paul's face down to his and they kissed. The taste of Paul's mouth, the feel of his lips and soft slick tongue, had become as familiar to Cory as his own heartbeat, and just as necessary. It made him feel warm and content.

It was several minutes before Cory could force himself from Paul's arms. "You better get going. Don't want to be late." He plucked at Paul's sticky shirt. "Better change first, though. Your mom may be an open-minded woman, but I'm betting this would be too much information."

Paul glanced down at himself and grimaced. "Yeah. Okay, let me get changed and I'll go. Sure you don't want to come with me?"

"I'm sure. You and your mom should have a little time alone. Besides," he hastily added as Paul opened his mouth to protest, "I've got dinner in the oven, I need to keep an eye on it."

Paul gave him a narrow look, but trotted into the bedroom without another word. Seconds later, he emerged wearing fresh jeans and a clean shirt. "Okay, I'm off. We'll be back in about an hour and a half."

"All right." Cory lifted his face for Paul's kiss. "Call me if you get tied up."

"I will. Love you."

"Love you too. Be careful."

Paul smiled, squeezed his hand, and hurried out the door.

Wandering into the bedroom to change his own clothes, Cory thought about the last few months. So much had happened in such a short time. He'd moved for the first time in his life. He'd sold the house he'd grown up in. He'd quit his job at Uncle Charlie's Porch and started full-time at Willow Bend Outdoors like he'd always wanted to do. He'd been through death and learning to trust and falling in love.

He'd lost his mother, and gained the love of a lifetime. Pain and happiness, one balancing the other. He couldn't find it in him to regret either.

He picked up the framed photo of himself and Paul on Otter Island, watching the sunset with their arms around each other. Alicia had taken the picture during a group outing, had it enlarged and framed, and given it to them for Christmas. Its twin hung on the living-room wall, a painting in soft watercolors. One of Paul's best, Cory thought. He smiled, brushing his fingers across the picture.

"Yes, Paul," he whispered. "I'm happy."

⊞ ⊞ ⊞

Paul arrived at baggage claim just as his mother stepped off the escalator from the concourse. He waved at her, and she waved back.

"Oh, my sweet baby!" she cried as Paul swept her into a hug. "It's so good to see you!"

"You too, Mom." He set her down and took her carry-on. "You look great."

"Flatterer." She smiled up at him as they walked toward the baggage carousel. "So do you, actually. Last time I saw you, you were too thin and you hadn't smiled in ages. You look happy now."

Paul returned her smile. "I am, Mom. Haven't been this happy since before Jay died."

She stopped and took his hand firmly in hers, blue-gray eyes very serious. "You love him, honey? And he loves you?"

"Yes, Mom." Paul smiled and kissed her cheek. "We love each other very much. We're happy together."

"That's all I need to know." She linked her arm through Paul's elbow. "Now let's get my suitcase. I'm anxious to meet this boy."

"He's anxious to meet you too." Paul patted his mother's hand as they went to join the crowd around the next to last carousel. "Just be gentle with him. He's so nervous I wouldn't be surprised if he exploded."

Cheryl laughed. "Sweetheart, I'll be the perfect mother-in-law, I promise. Oh, there's my bag, baby, will you get it? I can't lift the damn thing."

"I got it." Paul hefted the huge flowered suitcase and set it carefully on its built-in wheels. He took his mother's hand as they made their way out of the crowd. "I'm glad you're here, Mom."

"Me too, sweetie. Me too."

The ride back to the house went by quickly, Paul and Cheryl catching up on each other's lives. Listening to his mother's stories, he found that although he missed his family sometimes, he didn't miss Spokane. He'd always love it, and it would always be special to him, but he had a new home now. Here, with Cory.

The sun had nearly set when Paul pulled the truck into the barn. "Here we are," he said as they climbed out of the truck. "Home sweet home."

Cheryl looked around with obvious delight as they walked down the path to the house. "Paul, this is lovely!"

"Yeah, it is." Paul hauled the suitcase up the last stair and stood panting on the porch. "Damn. What've you got in here? Bricks?"

"Yes," she declared, straight-faced. Paul laughed.

They both turned when the door opened. Cory stood framed in the light of the open doorway. Paul's heart skipped a beat, as it always did when he saw his love. He hurried over, put an arm around Cory's shoulders, and kissed his forehead. He could feel Cory trembling.

"Mom, this is Cory Saunders. Cory, this is my mother, Cheryl Gordon."

Cory gave her a shy smile and held his hand out. "It's nice to meet you, Mrs. Gordon. I'm glad you could come."

Taking Cory's outstretched hand, Cheryl pulled him into a warm embrace. "None of that 'Mrs. Gordon' stuff, Cory. You're family. Call me Cheryl."

"Oh. Okay." Cory's voice was soft and shaky. He drew back, and this time his smile was the wide, slightly mischievous one Paul had fallen in love with. "Come on in, Cheryl. Dinner's just about ready."

"Wonderful, I'm starved." Cheryl took Cory's arm. "What're we having?"

"Veal parmesan, garlic bread and salad. And Chianti. I hope you like that, Paul said you would." Cory flashed a grin at Paul.

"Sounds delicious. And I love Chianti." Cheryl turned and winked at Paul. "Will you get my bags, honey? I'd like to talk to Cory for a little bit."

"Sure thing, Mom."

Paul caught Cory's eye as he grabbed his mother's bags. Those green eyes glowed. *I love you,* Cory mouthed silently. Paul smiled, and mouthed *I love you* back.

Cory and Cheryl were already chatting like old friends as they strolled through the open door into the house.

Paul turned, looking around at the darkened yard. The sweetness of the first spring flowers scented the cool, salty air. *This is my home*, he thought, with a burst of happiness. His home. His and Cory's. He'd come here to escape his old life, and ended up making a new one. It was more than he'd hoped for, and better than he'd ever dreamed.

Smiling, he followed his mother and his lover inside and shut the door.

Take a walk down the dark side of homoerotic literature
with this excerpt from...

BLOOD BROTHERS
© *2006 Barbara Sheridan and Anne Cain*

*Oh I know what he is to you, Liu, I can see the hunger
in your eyes for him. I felt the passion in your blood for him.
Even now you grow hard and ache for him and if I wasn't
here you'd be fucking him into the futon, wouldn't you?*

The trembling in Liu's hands worsened until his entire
body quivered. "I don't—I—," the young man gasped. He
kept the curved blade to Kuro's throat, but he sat back on
his heels and groaned. His free hand pressed against the
front of his *yukata*, stroking at the part in the robe
between his legs. Kuro laughed again when the steel
scraped against his neck, drawing out blood with the
same ease he'd drawn out the hidden desires of Liu's
heart. Kuro reached up and touched the boy's chin.

"Y—yes," Liu sighed heavily, his pulse quickening as
the blood rushed through his body with lust.

Give in to those desires... Kuro smiled, reaching out
with his senses until he could taste Kiyoshi's essence
through Liu's passionate imaginings.

"Gods!" Liu dropped the *kama* and scrambled
backwards away from Kuro. "How did you know that?" he
croaked. "Why can I hear your voice in my mind?"

"I am a strong man, Liu. Strong in ways you can't
even begin to imagine," Kuro said softly. "I can see inside

men to read what lies within their hearts." He sat up, leaning back on one elbow to regard Liu. "A farmer's life is not for you. Had you been born to better parents you would be a fine samurai. I sense in you a bloodthirsty warrior to rival the best Nobunaga's army has ever seen."

He stared at Liu, pleased by the way the young man's pulse quickened with excitement. Kuro sat up all the way and leaned forward. "I can make you a warrior, Liu. I can make you a man so strong that no one can defeat you, that no one will ever deny you what you want, be it a material thing or more intimate pleasures."

Kuro let his mind reach out again, pulling at the passion Liu felt for Kiyoshi. Kuro saw the images embedded in the young man's memory and drew them to the fore, adding his own power to make Liu squirm and bite back a moan of pent up desire.

"Stop it," Liu whimpered, but he reached down to pleasure himself with desperate strokes that matched his heaving breath. He brought himself to the verge of coming; Kuro could smell the musky scent on the young man's perspiration. Liu swallowed back another groan and pitched forward, resting on his palms. He moved towards Kuro, crawling on his hands and knees. "Leave us alone—we just want peace."

"Then why do you reach for the *kama* so quickly?" Kuro touched Liu's knuckles as the young man gripped the wooden handle of the curved scythe. "Your instinct is to take a farmer's tool for reaping crops and transform it into a weapon of death. It comes easily to you, doesn't it?"

Liu's eyes widened. He looked at Kuro's fingers as they brushed over his hand, his face twisting with confusion. "I want to be stronger," he admitted, seemingly for the first time. "I want Kiyo-kun to be stronger too. I—I want so many things. But he's happy here..."

"There are ways for you both to be happy." Kuro leaned forward, his lips just grazing Liu's ear. "Many ways. That I promise you."

"How?" Liu shivered, but the trembling in his body was from anticipation. "What are you?"

"I am the excitement you've always dreamed of. I am the giver of gifts you'll never encounter anywhere else."

Kuro's tongue snaked out and flicked along the edge of Liu's ear. The young man shuddered with pleasure pure enough for Kuro to taste. Smiling, he stroked Liu through the folds of the *yukata*.

Lie back, Liu. Lie back and let me taste the power I know you have.

Enjoy this nibble of a savory homoerotic delight...

TASTE THIS
© 2006 Leigh Ellwood

"Tobin." Kelly sounded exhausted. The baker's body was leaden and limp, like dragging a sack of Earth potatoes. "Tobin, I'm sorry, I never meant—"

"There's no reason to apologize, Kelly. You've done nothing wrong."

"You're acting as though I did."

"I am not!"

They breezed through the kitchen—rather, Tobin breezed and Kelly lagged. The aroma of baked chocolate and sweet sugared cake was faint, yet pleasant all the same. It did little, however, to overpower the tension.

"Your tone implies otherwise," Kelly said, stopping short of careening into Tobin.

"Kelly, I just want to talk. There's nothing sinister in that."

"We could have talked in the lounge."

Tobin frowned. So Kelly was eager to get back in there, was he? So he preferred Danae's pussy to his own hard, thick shaft?

Stop it. Tobin shook away the doubt and finally turned to Kelly, softening his expression to ease the worry in Kelly's.

"I want to talk in private, Kelly," he said quietly. "I haven't seen you all day, is all. I was hoping we could talk together like we normally do when I finish duty. I didn't find you in our quarters, so I tried here. That's when I checked the lounge."

"I see. I lingered a bit after my work was done, obviously," Kelly said. Tobin was unconvinced of Kelly's ease. The baker stiffened in his grip and looked around the kitchen as if expecting an ambush.

"Fine, we'll talk, but why are we at the pantry?" Kelly asked cautiously.

Tobin remained silent and gestured to the now open door. When Kelly hesitated, Tobin smiled. "I promise you, you'll come out alive," he said.

He escorted Kelly inside, engaging the lock behind them. Using the keypad by the door, he set the lighting at a minimal glow, leaving it light enough for them to move around without toppling any shelves. In this dark amber glow, Kelly appeared beautiful as ever. Curved shadows lent his profile a sensual air of mystery that Tobin found very arousing.

Tobin watched Kelly nervously pace a worn, circular path, and stroked his cock in silence. Kelly squinted in the dark at him, unaffected by the gesture.

"What are you going to do to me?"

"I want to make love to you, Kelly. I've tried to wait, tried to defer to your wishes, but it's getting more and more difficult to do."

"I thought we were going to talk."

"We just did."

Tobin tried to cross Kelly's path but backed away when the baker cast him a wide-eyed, worried frown.

Certainly he still didn't think Tobin brought him here to hurt him? Locking the door was meant to ensure privacy, not as a means to cut off escape.

"I'm sorry. You...you're just acting strange, is all. I can understand if you're upset with me..."

"I'm not, Kelly. You can do no wrong in my eyes, please understand that." Tobin pressed his two forefingers against the tip of his cock, supporting the rod as it stood to attention. "Look at this," he implored. "All I have to do is look at you and I'm hard as a rock. Do you have any idea what you do to me, Kelly?"

Kelly folded his arms over his chest, tucking his hands in his armpits. He looked down at his own limp cock, looking as though he should hide it away.

"That could come from anger, too," Kelly said, nodding at Tobin's erection.

"I'm not going to rape you," Tobin snapped. Oh, but Kelly tested him! Even as the baker frustrated him, Tobin remained aroused. If only he were a more eloquent man, able to better express his feelings. "You arouse me no matter what. Naked, clothed, baking, just sitting still...I can't get enough of you. I just want you to know that, and I want to show you how much it means to me."

"Were you turned on by what you saw?" Kelly's voice was weak, waiting for punishment. His hunched posture inferred expectation of a verbal lashing.

Tobin paused. What could he say? The scene was a shock, he had to admit. Over a week of lackluster oral sex from him, and he had to walk into the lounge to see Kelly enjoying it from both ends. Perplexing, yes, yet Tobin also had to acknowledge that seeing Kelly enjoy Wren's lips on his cock, and Danae tonguing his ass, was a turn-on. He said as much.

"Still," Kelly said when Tobin assured him of that, "you look mad enough to kill right now." He stopped pacing and stood in an aggressive pose, hands fisted at his sides. "So you know, I'll fight you if I have to. I could probably take you."

"I'm sure you could, but why would you? I don't want to fight, what makes you think I do?"

Kelly's hands relaxed. "I-I don't know. Part of me feels bad, and the other part defensive. I'm not sure what I should be doing."

"Besides talking?"

"Yes, but we're doing that now, aren't we?" Kelly forced a chuckle, but it hardly sounded amused. "I think this is the most we've talked in a while."

Tobin had to agree. The time following Kelly's arrival was parsed into a neat routine of work and sexual play and sleep. Tobin and Kelly, in particular, tended to work more then others on the *Jiu'Kr* simply because nobody existed to relieve them of their duties.

"I could come to like this, just talking," Kelly said. "Though I wish it didn't have to happen with you dragging me out of the lounge."

"Like I said, privacy. And you had the chance to resist me then, and still do now," Tobin pointed out, "yet you followed me like a child. In fact, you were the most confident at Taste This. Here, not so much, and I can't understand why. You're on even footing."

"Taste This was the home field advantage," Kelly said. "That was home—"

Tobin's heart plummeted at this. Would the *Jiu'Kr* ever be home?

Samhain Publishing, Ltd.

It's all about the story…

Action/Adventure
Fantasy
Historical
Horror
Mainstream
Mystery/Suspense
Non-Fiction
Paranormal
Red Hots!
Romance
Science Fiction
Western
Young Adult

http://www.samhainpublishing.com

Printed in the United States
56822LVS00008B/19-21